"*Mrs. Crenshaw, ah...*"

Hope had never seen a big man look so sheepish.

"I...ah, I've got some business in Havre tomorrow," Pete said. "And, well, I was wondering, that is, if you're not too busy..." He paused and took a deep breath. "Guess you can tell I'm not real good at this sort of thing. But I'm trying to ask if you'll ride into Havre with me and take some dinner."

Hope experienced a surge of joy so deep she wondered if it was showing on her face. She wanted to go with him more than she'd wanted anything in a long, long time.

It was out of the question, of course. The less time she spent with Pete Hamilton, the less likely he was to stumble onto her secret.

But it didn't seem fair. The loneliness in his eyes was so real—and she knew what it was like to feel lonely. Surely there was no harm in having one dinner with the man....

Dear Reader,

Welcome to Silhouette—experience the magic of the wonderful world where two people fall in love. Meet heroines that will make you cheer for their happiness, and heroes (be they the boy next door or a handsome, mysterious stranger) who will win your heart. Silhouette Romance reflects the magic of love—sweeping you away with books that will make you laugh and cry, heartwarming, poignant stories that will move you time and time again.

In the coming months we're publishing romances by many of your all-time favorites, such as Diana Palmer, Brittany Young, Sondra Stanford and Annette Broadrick. Your response to these authors and our other Silhouette Romance authors has served as a touchstone for us, and we're pleased to bring you more books with Silhouette's distinctive medley of charm, wit and—above all—*romance*.

I hope you enjoy this book and the many stories to come. Experience the magic!

Sincerely,

Tara Hughes
Senior Editor
Silhouette Books

NORA POWERS

Woman of the West

Silhouette *Romance*

Published by Silhouette Books New York

America's Publisher of Contemporary Romance

For Dave and Ginny
with love

SILHOUETTE BOOKS
300 E. 42nd St., New York, N.Y. 10017

Copyright © 1989 by Nora Powers

ISBN: 0-373-08637-7

First Silhouette Books printing March 1989

All the characters in this book are fictitious. Any
resemblance to actual persons, living or dead, is
purely coincidental.

®: Trademark used under license and
registered in the United States Patent and
Trademark Office and in other countries.

Printed in the U.S.A.

NORA POWERS

has written a dozen books for Silhouette, and this is the fourth set in Montana. She confesses to a passion for that state, as well as for horses and the American West in general. She finds writing almost as necessary as breathing and strongly believes that love is our reason for being.

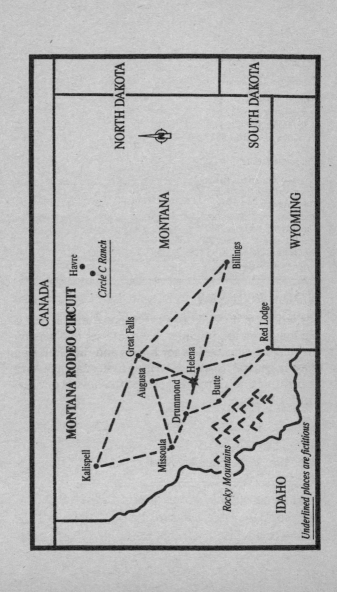

MONTANA RODEO CIRCUIT

CANADA

NORTH DAKOTA

SOUTH DAKOTA

MONTANA

WYOMING

IDAHO

Havre

Circle C Ranch

Great Falls

Kalispell

Augusta

Missoula

Drummond

Helena

Butte

Billings

Red Lodge

Rocky Mountains

Underlined places are fictitious

Chapter One

The bull had mean eyes. Mean black eyes that peered from folds of coarse brown flesh.

Less than six feet away, Hope Crenshaw swallowed. Only trampled sawdust separated her from one of the most dangerous bulls on the Montana circuit. Pungent arena dust stung her nostrils, gritted between her half-clenched teeth.

She tugged at the bright red suspenders, hitched up the baggy blue pants, put a hand to the curly yellow wig. Why? she thought. Why did she ever think she wanted to do this?

The bull snorted, wide wet nostrils flaring in rage. He shook the wicked curved horns that could kill a man—or a woman, for that matter—with one properly placed thrust. The ugly folds beneath his neck swayed as he swung his huge head from side to side.

Off to his left, the downed rider lay in the sawdust. Dazed. Unable to move.

Hope's heart pounded in her chest. She was afraid. But, she told herself, it was a fear she could handle. Remember what Clint always said—you're smarter than this bull, than any bull.

"Yah! Yah!" Hope danced toward the animal, waving her arms. She spun on her heel, flicking a bright orange handkerchief in his eyes.

The Augusta crowd roared its approval as the bull pawed the ground and lunged toward her. Making a tight little circle, Hope evaded him. From the corner of her eye she saw young Charlie Rivers reach the safety of the fence and scramble up it.

Swallowing a sigh of relief, Hope danced this way and that, getting ever closer to the bull. He tossed his wicked horns again and then, shaking his head once more, trotted out through the open gate.

"And that," said the announcer's deep voice, "ends the bullriding events for today. How about a nice hand for our clown, Hobie Brown? He's a little fellow, but he's sure got what it takes. Yes sir, old Hobie's faster than a speeding bullet. Well, anyway, he's faster than the rankest bull."

Hope smiled to herself. Hearing Pete's deep voice always made her feel warm and good inside. Even though he thought he was talking about Hobie the clown and not the woman he knew as Hope Crenshaw, his voice gave her a tremendous lift.

Hope bobbed in acknowledgment as the audience laughed and applauded. Then, as she usually did at this point, she pretended to trip over her own feet.

The crowd was still laughing as she swaggered out through the gate and headed back behind the chutes. Thank God, Old Devil Eyes had been the last bull on today's draw. Hitching up her baggy pants once more, she allowed herself to think of the luxury of a hot shower and the quiet of a peaceful motel room.

"Good job, Hobie," Charlie Rivers called down to her from the top fence rail.

His youth and his blond hair always made her think of Matt. Someday soon her son would be grown. He might even look a lot like this young cowboy.

"You're welcome," she called, her naturally deep voice carrying.

"Thought he was gonna get me today," Charlie said, grinning.

"Old Devil Eyes is the right name for him," Hope replied, waving to him as she continued on her way.

Yes, she'd never said anything truer. But she'd handled him, just the way Clint had taught her. A lump formed in her throat at the thought of her late husband.

The arena always brought back memories of the old days, memories of the times they'd worked together, two funny-faced baggy-pants clowns, chasing the bulls, making audiences roar with laughter.

How Clint had loved the circuit. He'd loved everything about the rodeo—the screaming, yelling, applauding crowds, the mingled smells of popcorn, leather, horses and manure and, most of all, the challenge of his work.

He would grin one of those brash grins she'd loved so much and say, "When I'm nose-to-nose with one of those sons of guns, why, then I know I'm alive."

And now he wasn't. Hope swallowed painfully.

She flexed her aching shoulders. God, she was tired. Each separate nerve seemed to quiver when she was waiting for the welcome sound of the qualifying buzzer. She was sure she was just as relieved as the bullrider when the eight seconds were over and he could let go of his rope, jump to the ground and skedaddle up the fence to safety.

She sighed again. "Going on down the road," as rodeo people called it, wasn't an easy life. Constantly on the move and living out of suitcases, bone-weary cowboys climbed into their trucks at the end of the day to drive long miles to the next town. The next night they did it all over again, on a circuit that seemed to go on endlessly. It was no life for a homebody, but in spite of its hardships, many people loved it.

Anyhow, a good hot shower would take most of the ache out of her muscles. Luckily for her, she didn't have to worry about taking care of stock before heading homeward.

She made sure the motel corridor was empty before she unlocked the door and slipped inside her room. Hobie Brown, rodeo clown, was about to become Hope Crenshaw again. She unpinned the yellow wig and tossed it onto the bed. Her own long dark hair lay coiled in a braid around her head. She left it there while she slid down the suspenders and climbed out of the baggy blue pants and the red-and-white polka-dot shirt.

The red tennis shoes were the only part of the costume that wasn't oversize. Clint had always been serious about shoes. "Your costume can be anything you want," he would say when they talked to schoolkids about rodeo clowning. "But don't funny up your shoes. Your life depends on being able to move fast."

Hope slid out of her cotton panties and the bra that held her small breasts close to her body and headed for the shower.

As the hot water beat down on her, she swallowed a sudden sob. Clint was still so real to her, so alive. She could see his face, could almost hear his voice.

It hardly seemed possible that two whole years had passed since the awful day she'd opened the door to the state troopers. It was a nightmarish repeat of the time they'd come to tell her about her parents, both dead in an accident on the interstate. But this time it had been Clint.

Her beloved Clint, who had survived so many dangers in the arena, had been struck down by a hit-and-run driver. At least it had been quick. No pain, the troopers had told her. By the looks of it, death had been instantaneous.

It had felt like her death, too. So much of her had gone with him. It would have been easy just to give up. But there had been Matthew to think about. An eight-year-old who'd lost his adored father needed his mother more than ever.

So she'd stuck it out. Through the lonely, pain-filled nights, through the long, weary days of ranch work, clinging to Clint's mother's promise that it would get better.

Hope shifted so that the water hit the sore spot beneath her right shoulder blade. Mom Crenshaw had been right. It *had* gotten better. Some. The heartache wasn't so bad anymore, and she slept most nights now—or she had until they'd lost Sultan.

The bull had sired some prize stock, and his stud fees had been a big part of the ranch's income, but he hadn't been much on brains. And when a sudden cloudburst had caught him in a dry wash, the raging, tumbling water had swept away the Circle C's secure future. For it was those stud fees that had made the difference between red ink and black for the ranch that she and Clint had so lovingly built.

Hope stepped out of the shower and toweled her small, firm body. Two weeks on the circuit had already toughened it. She didn't ache as much or in as many places. Hobie Brown was doing a good job as a rodeo clown. Though she hardly dared believe it, Mom Crenshaw's crazy scheme was actually working!

She slipped into her jeans and shirt, loosened the long braid and brushed out her hair. She always took care to look as feminine as possible when she wasn't wearing her clown getup. She also always had her excuse ready if she happened to run into Pete Hamilton.

For a moment her heart beat faster. It seemed incredible that just three weeks ago Pete Hamilton had been only a name out of Clint's past. As she ran the brush through her long, smooth hair, Hope remembered the discussion with Clint's Mom, the discussion that had finally taken her to Pete's Helena office.

"It's not fair, them not letting you work." Claire Crenshaw's lined forehead had been furrowed with worry. "You got the credentials from when you worked with Clint. But you know how those cowboys are. You look as fragile as fine china." She'd wrinkled her pert nose and snorted delicately. "Too dangerous, indeed."

Hope sighed. She'd been over and over it. "I've got to do something. And a typing job, even if I can find one, won't pay enough."

Claire frowned. "Why, I've known women could outrope any man. In the old rodeo days my mama used to do anything the cowboys did. And usually better."

"I've just got to convince this Hamilton." Hope paced the big kitchen's worn linoleum. "I've already been turned down too many times. We've got to replace that bull."

"I know, Hope honey. But it don't look so good. Unless . . ." A sly look crossed Claire's sun-darkened face.

Hope knew that look. Sometimes Claire's ideas were almost more than she could handle. But sometimes . . . "Unless what?"

Claire grinned. "Unless you let him think you're a man."

Hope stopped her pacing and stared at her mother-in-law. "A man? How can I do that?"

"Well, clowns wear some pretty crazy getups. Those big floppy clothes. Paint all over their faces."

"And funny wigs." Hope nodded. "But what about the credentials? You know I've got to have two recommendations from other bullfighting clowns. And one from a stock director."

Claire frowned. "Let me think."

Hope sighed again. Sometimes she wished she'd been hit along with Clint that fatal day. It was selfish, she knew. But since his death the ranch had faced one problem after another, and they'd all been up to her to solve—her, a woman born and raised in the city.

Her mother-in-law smiled. "This fellow you're going to be can tell Pete Hamilton he trained with Clint." She grinned. "I'll talk to Willie Sutton and Hank Shreves. Fred Burns, too. They were old Matt's buddies. They'll help us even though he's gone."

Hope nodded. Clint's father's friends had certainly done everything they could to help. But this...this was an awful lot to ask.

"I'll explain it to them," Claire went on. "After all, they gave you recommendations as your own self. And far as I remember there's no space on the form that asks for your sex. So you won't be telling any lies."

Hope shook her head. Sometimes Claire got carried away with her ideas. And this scheme sounded awfully chancy. "But will that help? Will someone hire a man as small as me?"

Her mother-in-law smiled. "Don't worry, honey. Many's the time I heard Clint talk about Hamilton. He always said he was one of the most fair-minded men around." She smiled at Hope. "Anyhow, it's worth a try. You just think up a man's name for yourself and I'll take care of the rest."

So Hope swallowed her scruples and made an appointment with Pete Hamilton's office. As soon as she got into Helena she found a gas station where she could put on her outfit. The broad, bright lines of makeup and the curly yellow wig really made a good disguise. And the baggy, outsize shirt and pants hid her slight feminine curves. But she was still nervous. So much was riding on this—the whole future of the Circle C.

Standing there in front of Pete Hamilton's desk, Hope studied the rodeo promoter. He reminded her of a brown bear. He was big, and his bushy mustache and unruly brown hair, as well as the curling brown wisps peeking over the open top button of his plaid shirt, contributed to the picture.

But bears didn't have wide shoulders and flat bellies. Or bright blue eyes. And they certainly didn't make a woman feel so undeniably feminine, especially a woman whose gender was hidden under paint and baggy clothes.

"So you're looking for a job." Pete Hamilton looked the clown over carefully. There was something different about this one. He couldn't quite put his finger on it, but something stirred in the back of his mind when he looked at him.

The voice was big, kind of gravelly, but everything else was small. Delicate-looking, almost. And those wide brown eyes, with their long, thick lashes—they should have belonged to a woman.

Maybe that was it. Something about this fellow seemed womanish. His smallness, maybe.

Well, a man couldn't help his size. Hiking his feet up onto the desktop, Pete looked the man over. "Kinda small, aren't you?"

The clown stiffened and stuck out his chin. "I don't aim to *tackle* the bull," he replied. "Clint—Mr. Crenshaw—he said I was real good. One of the best he'd ever seen."

"Is that so?" Pete wasn't a suspicious man, but he liked to take his time, to think things through. And there was something here that wasn't quite right.

"Clint Crenshaw's been gone two years," he said. "Where've you been?"

The fellow swallowed and gnawed on his lower lip. He seemed a little on the nervous side.

"Just before it happened I had to go back to Miles City," he said, pulling at the red suspenders. "Pa died and Ma needed me. But I've been keeping at it— practicing."

Pete leaned back, boots still propped up on the scarred desk, and contemplated a steeple made of his fingertips. There was something . . .

"I've got credentials," the fellow said, shifting from one foot to the other.

Pete looked his papers over. And then it came to him. The niggling little something in the back of his mind popped right out where he could see it.

When he'd been calling around, asking about another clown, he'd heard about one looking for work, a woman, Clint Crenshaw's widow. And now, funny thing, here was Hobie Drown, a fellow he'd never heard of who had supposedly been trained by Clint and who was carrying credentials from friends of Clint's daddy. It seemed quite a coincidence.

If Crenshaw's widow wanted to face the bulls, she must need the money bad. If he remembered right, she wasn't rodeo born or bred. There'd been a while they'd clowned together, after she'd talked her man out of riding the bulls.

But Clint had said she didn't like clowning that much. And she'd quit when their boy had started school. That ranch of theirs must be having trouble for her to go back to it now.

He could see why the others had turned her down. She looked fragile even in the garish clown outfit. "'Fraid she'll get hurt," one man had said. "A woman like that oughtta stay home," said another.

Pete Hamilton stared into space. He'd liked Clint Crenshaw, admired him. And though he'd never met his wife, he'd seen the man's joy in her. Now Clint was gone. And here stood his widow.

At least he was pretty sure it was her. Clint's widow, needing work and unable to get it. That was a dirty shame.

Well, Pete had always been a sucker for the underdog. And what harm could it do? If it wasn't Clint's widow, well, this fellow still needed work, and he needed a clown.

"I could use another clown," he said slowly. "One of my regulars left last month."

Hope bit down on her trembling lower lip, then quickly released it. That wasn't a manly thing to do. She tried to think how Clint would handle this. "I'd be glad to do a show first and sign a contract after you've seen me work."

Hamilton nodded. "Sounds fair enough. Thing is, I've got nothing but your word that you worked with Clint. Not that it isn't good, but you being a stranger and all... If there was just someone around to back you up."

Hope took a deep breath. "Guess you could ask his missus. I reckon she'd remember me."

Pete Hamilton smiled. It was a warm smile that stirred something inside Hope and made her want to smile, too. She closed her mouth firmly. Hobie Brown shouldn't be given to smiling too easy.

"That's a right good idea. You just give me your number. I'll check with Mrs. Crenshaw and get back to you."

"I-I'm on the road," she stammered. "Don't have a place of my own yet. How about I call you? Say Thursday?"

Pete lowered his worn boots to the floor and got to his feet. She rose, too, and as she did she noticed how he towered over her. He extended his hand. "Done," he said firmly. "I'll expect your call. Thanks for stopping by."

His handclasp was as strong and firm as Clint's had been the first time she'd met him. She felt a tingle of warmth travel up her arm and race through the rest of her body.

Hamilton went with her to the door. "Take care now, Hobie."

As she made her way down the hall, she heard him say, "Martha, get me the number of Clint Crenshaw's widow. Over Havre way."

Chapter Two

Yes, Hope thought as she stowed her suitcase in the back of the ranch wagon, her first meeting with Pete Hamilton had been interesting, all right. But the second had been even more so.

After the appointment she'd rushed out to find a phone to call home and warn Claire. But when she'd reached her mother-in-law she'd found that Pete had already called.

"I told him to come by tomorrow," Claire had said. "Figured you'd want to get it over with."

The next day, ready long before the appointed time, Hope had been nervously pacing the kitchen again.

"You're going to wear a hole in that floor," her

mother-in-law said. "Calm down. You've fought bulls. You can handle this."

She ran appraising eyes over her daughter-in-law. "You look real good."

"Mom! This isn't a fashion show!"

Claire grinned. "Honey, men like to see a pretty woman. And Pete Hamilton is a man."

Hope felt the red rise to her cheeks. Hamilton was a man, all right. She wished she weren't quite so aware of that. It had been a long time since she'd been affected this way by a man.

She fidgeted and began her pacing again. It made sense to look as feminine as possible. She ought to look different from Hobie Brown. But the blouse and skirt made her feel strange, and so did having her hair hang loose down her back. She was not a woman given to dressing up, and she seldom wore skirts or dresses.

She only hoped all this effort wasn't wasted. If Hamilton recognized her as Hobie, their plan would be ruined before it began.

They heard his pickup pull into the yard, and Claire gave her a quick hug. "Remember," she said. "Just be yourself."

Hope had to swallow twice before she found the courage to open the door. Standing there on the front porch, Pete Hamilton looked even bigger than he had in his office—even bigger, and even more male. His smile was still as warm, with white, even teeth showing under the bushy mustache.

He was a sight to lighten any woman's heart in his jeans and his blue silk shirt, his black boots gleaming in the sunlight.

He took off his worn Stetson. "Afternoon, Mrs. Crenshaw. Nice of you to see me on such short notice."

"It's no trouble. Come on in." She tried to control her lower lip. This was no time for it to be trembling.

He followed her into the living room, hat in hand.

"Sit down. Be comfortable." She waved a vague hand toward the furniture but, though he moved toward a chair, he didn't sit down until she did.

"Mom's making lemonade," Hope said. She felt foolish, like a girl on her first date. Why had Claire had to bring up all that silly stuff about pretty women? This was strictly business. Or at least it should be. "Sorry, we don't have anything stronger to offer you."

Pete forced himself to smile. "Won't bother me," he said. "I gave up liquor a while back. Didn't agree with my wallet or my head. Lemonade sounds just fine."

He watched the woman. He was almost positive now. There *could* be two gravelly voices like that. Maybe. But the way she worried her lower lip with those little white teeth...that was just what Hobie had done in his office the day before.

She sure looked different. Still fragile. And real pretty. But looks didn't matter. Since Clint had trained her, he had no doubt she could do the job. Fred Burns wouldn't have recommended her if he'd doubted her ability. It wasn't fair to shut her out just because of her size—or her sex.

He caught himself wondering how she would fit in his arms. Damn fool, he told himself sharply. Was he forgetting Annie already? Hadn't that wife of his taught him anything?

Still, a man got lonesome, and nothing more than a little companionship had to come of it. But he hadn't come here to make calf's eyes at Crenshaw's widow. He'd come to see if the woman needed work.

Across from him, Hope felt another pang of guilt. Pete Hamilton seemed like such a nice man. It didn't seem fair to bamboozle him. But it wasn't as if she couldn't do the job. She was as good as any rodeo clown alive. Clint had told her so.

She certainly wasn't trying to save the ranch for purely selfish reasons. It was Matt's inheritance—all he had left of his father. Besides, none of this would have been necessary if the rest of the rodeo clan hadn't closed ranks and been so set on "protecting" her.

"So, how are things going?" Hamilton's bright blue eyes took in everything in the living room of the ranch house, from the Navaho rugs on the polished oak floors to the reproduction of the Charlie Russell painting *The Challenge* over the huge stone fireplace.

"Pretty good," Hope said. "We lost our prize bull a while back. But other than that we're doing okay."

Hamilton nodded. "Place looks good. Real good." He paused. "Well, I'd best get down to business. A fellow came to me yesterday—Hobie Brown."

He stopped, and she forced herself to nod casually. "Yes, I remember him."

Hamilton's eyes watched her closely, gauging her reaction. "He says he worked with Clint, learning clowning from him."

Hope nodded again. "That's right."

"Scrawny kind of fellow, this Hobie. Not much meat on his bones."

Why did men always judge everything by size? "I remember him as real light on his feet," she said. "Is he in some kind of trouble?"

Hope was pleased with that question. After all, she wasn't supposed to know why Hamilton was there.

He shook his head and crossed one big leg over the other. "Nope. He wants a job clowning, and I thought I ought to check his story out." He turned the worn Stetson over in his hands.

She should have taken it from him, she realized. In her nervousness she'd forgotten to be polite.

"And now that you've confirmed Clint trained him," Hamilton continued, "I reckon I can take him on."

Hope's heart jumped joyfully up into her throat. But she kept her face carefully composed and her hands quiet in her lap. "I hope he works out for you."

"I expect he will."

Claire chose that moment to enter with the lemonade. After introductions had been made and she'd returned to the kitchen, Pete Hamilton leaned back in his chair. "Good lemonade. Bet Mrs. Crenshaw's a fine cook."

Hope nodded. "Yes, she is. I'm lucky to have her here."

He nodded, sipping slowly.

The silence in the room grew. Hope searched her mind for a safe topic of conversation, but her wits seemed to have failed her. She could think of nothing but how strange it seemed to have an attractive man sitting in her living room. A man who wasn't Clint, that is. A man she was attracted to. It was a new thought, and she examined it, still unable to think of any way to get a conversation going.

Pete uncrossed his legs, crossed them again, then uncrossed them. He took a big swallow of lemonade. And suddenly he was choking and coughing.

Hope was on her feet instantly, gripping his shoulder with one hand and pounding him on the back with the other.

It wasn't until after he'd stopped coughing and she'd lingered at his side that she realized what she was doing. She had ahold of a stranger, a male stranger.

She was still standing there, her hand on his shoulder, bemused by the fact that touching him felt so good, when he turned to look up at her. His blue eyes were warm, and she smelled the good male scent of horses, worn leather and sage.

"Thank you kindly," he said.

The words were simple ones, but Hope felt the red flooding her face. She felt a sudden urge to bend and kiss the upturned face. She wanted to feel his arms around her, drawing her close. Appalled that she should be having such thoughts, she pulled her fingers back from the warmth of his flesh.

"You think quick," he said, admiration in his voice. "I like that in a woman."

There was something in his tone, something warmer than anything Hope had heard there before. It kept her face flushed, made her breathing come a little faster.

Hurriedly she returned to her chair. "When you have children, Mr. Hamilton, you have to know what to do."

"Of course. There's the boy. Matthew, isn't it?"

She nodded. "Yes. He's ten."

Again there was silence. Silence that went on and on. She had to think of something to talk about. Something...

"Mrs. Crenshaw, ah..."

She'd never seen a big man look so sheepish.

"I...ah, I've got some business in Havre tomorrow," he said. "And, well, a man in my line of work gets lonesome. I don't often get to spend time with a pretty woman. And I was wondering, that is, if you're not too busy. . ."

He paused and took a deep breath. "Guess you can tell I'm not real good at this sort of thing. But I'm trying to ask you if you'll ride into Havre with me and take some dinner."

Hope experienced a surge of joy so deep she wondered if it was showing on her face. She wanted to go with him more than she'd wanted anything in a long, long time.

It was out of the question, of course. The less time she spent with Pete Hamilton, the less likely he was to stumble onto her secret.

But it didn't seem fair. The loneliness in his eyes was so real. It hurt to feel like that. She knew how it hurt. And Pete Hamilton *had* helped her. Shouldn't she do something for him in return? Surely there was no harm in having one dinner with the man.

Before she'd thought it all through, she found herself saying, "I believe I could do that, Mr. Hamilton."

His anxious look was replaced by that warm smile she was already growing to love. "Thank you kindly. This'll be a real treat for me. And a bigger one if you'll call me Pete."

Hope smiled. "Only if you call me Hope."

Three weeks, Hope thought, as the miles of prairie sped by beneath the wagon's tires. Only three weeks since she'd first sat across that table from Pete Hamilton.

It had been an evening she'd thought about many times since. They'd spent the evening talking—about ranching, about rodeoing. About Clint. Easily and naturally Pete had told her how much he'd respected Clint and his work.

"It used to make me jealous," he'd admitted with another sheepish grin. "The way he talked about his wonderful woman." He'd chuckled. "There were times I didn't believe the son of a gun. He's putting me on, I told myself. No woman in the West is that good."

He inched his hand across the table and touched hers, so lightly, so swiftly it was gone before she knew it had come. "But now that I've met you, I see Clint was telling it true."

Hope felt herself flushing again. A man like Pete deserved respect. Respect and true dealing. And what was he getting from her? She pushed the thought away.

His deep laugh rang out when she ordered her steak "burned to a crisp" and to her complete surprise he told the smiling waitress, "Make mine the same."

Seeing Hope's quizzical expression, he grinned. "I always like to try new things."

Unexpected warmth curled through her. *Careful,* she told herself, *you're not used to keeping company*

with a man. She had to be very careful with this man—
more careful than with all the others.

The steaks arrived without a trace of pink but tender and succulent nevertheless.

He shook his head. "Never thought well-done could
taste that good."

Hope smiled. "They know me here." She didn't tell
him that this had been one of their favorite places, hers
and Clint's. Somehow tonight there was no pain, only
the feel of comforting memories.

But he had seen something in her expression. His
ruddy face turned serious. "You used to come here
together. You and Clint."

"Yes."

"You should have told me. We could have gone
somewhere else."

Hope shook her head. "No, I didn't want to. I
wanted to come here."

His eyes were so warm, so comforting. "Thank
you," he said. "For sharing this place with me. Like
I said, a man gets lonesome eating alone."

"Are you often alone?" She realized too late that it
was a leading question, but she felt a real need to
know.

"'Fraid so." His face grew closed, his eyes cloudy.

Hope hesitated. There had been a wife, she remembered distantly. If only she could remember what had
happened to her.

"Loneliness is bad," she agreed.

He shook himself slightly and gave her a little smile. "Will you listen to this dumb cowboy? Here I am, acting as if you didn't know a thing about it." His eyes grew dark with sympathy. "You've been hurting, too." Again he reached across the table to touch her hand. It was a warm, comforting touch.

She wanted to give comfort in return, but she didn't know how. "Mom says it gets better. With time."

He didn't look at all sure. "I reckon Mrs. Crenshaw's a wise lady. You'd do good to listen to her."

This time Hope reached across the table and covered his hand with hers. "You're still a young man," she said softly. "You can love again, marry again."

He opened his hand slowly and enclosed her own. Only then did Hope realize the implication of her words.

"I don't think so," he said. "I don't think I'm the marrying kind."

Hope pulled into the yard at the ranch and sat for a moment, her head bowed wearily over the wheel, before climbing out. Why would a man like Pete say a thing like that? She'd puzzled over it night and day for the past three weeks, but she was no closer to an answer than she had been that evening.

The sound of approaching hooves broke the stillness, and she turned to look out toward the back range. Matt came galloping through the yard and pulled his pinto to a sliding halt. "Hi, Mom."

"Hi, honey." Hope swallowed a sudden lump in her throat. Matt had his father's dark eyes and towhead. And his winning smile. "I see you've been out riding."

Matt jumped from the saddle and ran to give her a big hug. "Yeah, Hank says I can ride during fall roundup."

Hope returned his hug. "As long as you don't miss any school."

"Aw, Mom."

Hope held her son off and looked at him sternly. "Clint Matthew Crenshaw, you know how your daddy felt about school. You need that learning." She smiled. "Grandma and I are counting on you to run the ranch when we get old."

A cloud of fear settled on her son's features, and he rushed back into her arms, hugging her fiercely.

A shiver knifed down Hope's spine. Matt was still hurting over his father's death. "It's okay, honey," she said soothingly. "I'm going to be around a long time."

As she hugged him to her, a picture of Old Devil Eyes rose up to taunt her.

Hope pushed the image away. Clint had always insisted that clowning was the safest of all rodeo activities. Otherwise he wouldn't have let her do it with him.

Her city background had made her fearful at first, but he'd laughed and said, "There's nothing to fall off of, honey. And I'm smarter than any damn bull. No matter how rank the critter is."

She could still see him standing there, his hands on his hips, grinning like a little boy with a new toy, before he'd scooped her up in his arms and swung her around the room.

Hope hugged his son closer. It might have been that very night that Matt had been conceived.

She forced her thoughts away from Clint. As his mother so often pointed out, there was no sense in dwelling on things, especially things that hurt so much.

Hope meant to change the subject, but she was interrupted by the ringing of the telephone. Matt pulled loose and tore into the house. "Jimmy's supposed to call," he yelled back over his shoulder.

Hope winced as the weathered screen slammed behind him. But then boys were always noisy. She shrugged and started up the worn wooden stairs. Clint's mother would be in the kitchen, no doubt.

And that was where she found her, up to her elbows in soapy dishwater. Hope picked up a towel. "I thought Matt was supposed to help."

Claire chuckled. "That boy breaks more dishes than he dries. Besides, he needs to be out with the menfolk." She looked at Hope and frowned. "And you need to sit down."

"I've been sitting," Hope protested. "Driving's not hard work."

"'Course not." Clint's mother snorted. "And chasing 'round in the arena with mean-eyed monsters is no more tiring than baking a cake! Fiddlesticks, child. Any fool can see you're worn out."

She wiped her soapy hands on her huge, comfortable apron. "You leave the dishes be. They'll dry just as well by themselves. Supposed to be healthier, too."

Hope smiled. "I don't know what we'd do without you. All this cooking. And taking care of Matt while I'm away."

"Been cooking and watching kids all my grown life," Claire said complacently. "And I mean to keep on doing it long as I'm alive. I always pull my own weight."

"Even more," Hope said quietly. She knew that without this sturdy little woman's help the Circle C would already have been lost.

"He called," Claire said. "That Hamilton fellow. I told him you were out doing errands." She shook her graying head. "I sure hope God doesn't hold me to account for the lies I've been telling lately."

Hope forced a chuckle and tried to look unconcerned. "I hope so, too."

Her nonchalance wasn't real, of course. Joy was bubbling up inside her. All the way home, even out there on the porch with Matt, the question had been in the back of her mind. Had Pete called? *Would* he call?

Their first dinner had ended with a simple handshake, and Hope had felt the rightness of that. But she'd also felt the rightness when Pete had said, "I'd like to call you sometime, Hope."

And now the call she'd been waiting for had finally come.

Chapter Three

Hope smiled as she made her way to the den. It seemed strange to be waiting for a call from a man. There had never been anyone for her but Clint. He'd been the first man she'd ever loved—the only one, actually.

He had been just eighteen, an unknown on the road for his first season. That was probably the only reason a shy sixteen-year-old like herself had had the nerve to approach a rodeo bullrider. She still had the autograph he'd given her that day in Glasgow, an illegible signature scrawled across a tattered program. Someday she would give it to Matt and tell him how she'd met his father.

She opened the door to the den, and her son jumped guiltily and took his boots off the scarred desk. "Gotta go, Jim. Talk to you later."

Hope made no comment about the boots. Clint had always sat that way, his feet propped high. It was natural for Matt to do the same.

"Thanks, Matt. I've got a call to make."

"Yeah, I know." Matt was already headed out the door. "I'm going to take a ride."

Hope nodded. "See you later."

As she sank into the battered chair she wished she knew what her son was thinking and feeling.

They spoke of Clint—the three of them—easily and often, recalling good times. And it had been almost a year since Matt had blurted out, "Oh, Mom, I miss him so much," and she'd held him while they'd both cried.

Matt was growing up fast, growing away from her, learning to keep his feelings to himself.

She sighed. She wished he wouldn't hang out with Hank and the cowhands so much. But he was a boy and he needed to be around men.

Hope reached for the phone. She was grateful to Clint's widowed mother for her help through these trying months. Without her, she didn't think she could have made it.

But somehow she'd never expected to hear Claire say, as she had just the other day, "Hope Elizabeth

Crenshaw, it's time you were seeing other men. I like this Pete Hamilton. And I think you do, too."

She dialed the unfamiliar number. The phone rang three times. Maybe he was gone. Maybe she'd missed him for the evening.

"Hello, Pete Hamilton here."

At the sound of his deep voice, Hope's heart jumped a little. She heard him every day when they worked, but now the warmth was especially for her. She smiled as the tiredness of the long drive slipped away.

"Hello, Pete. This is Hope. Sorry I missed your call."

"Have you eaten yet?"

"No, I just got in."

"Good. I'm in Havre unexpected. Want to have dinner?"

The sudden racing of her heart told her how glad she was. But there was her secret to think of. She probably shouldn't go, shouldn't spend time with him as Hope. That was asking to be discovered.

She opened her mouth to give him some excuse and heard herself say, "Yes, thank you. I'd like that."

"Great. Can you be ready in half an hour?"

"Yes." It was probably insanity, but she couldn't help it. She wanted to be with him again, wanted to feel the warmth of his smile. Surely one more dinner wouldn't hurt, one more pleasant evening.

She put the receiver down and hurried to the kitchen. "Pete'll be here in half an hour. We're going to dinner."

Claire nodded. "You just hightail it upstairs and get ready. Wear something pretty."

Hope swallowed over the lump in her throat and crossed the kitchen to hug her. "You're a wonderful lady," she whispered.

"Horsefeathers!" Claire's embarrassed reaction was instantaneous, but her eyes were suspiciously bright. "I'm not so old I've lost my good sense! A woman your age needs a man." She laughed. "And that Pete's a good one. If I was a little younger I might even try to rope him myself." She grinned and waved her apron at Hope. "Go on, now. Hustle."

Twenty minutes later Hope came down the stairs wearing her blue denim prairie skirt and a ruffled blue-and-lilac plaid blouse. "Have you seen my good boots?" she asked, twirling for Claire's inspection.

"Over there in the corner," Claire said, waving a wet hand. "I polished them this afternoon. After he called."

"He told you?"

Claire shook her head. "No, honey. I heard it in his voice. Men are funny. Lovable, but funny. They think they're so big and strong. And that they know every-thing." She winked. "But most of the time they aren't half as smart as they think."

She glanced out the window that faced the road. "For instance, this one can't even tell time. He's ten minutes early."

Turning, Hope saw the dust cloud that meant someone was coming up the lane. "Well, I guess I'm ready."

Claire nodded. "You relax and have a good time. You deserve it. And don't you worry about Matt. I've got my eye on him."

"Thanks, Mom."

Pete was already halfway up the front steps when Hope opened the door. Happiness flooded over her as he took the last two steps in a bound and stopped in front of her, his eyes full of warmth.

For a crazy moment she wanted to walk right up to him, throw her arms around his neck and raise her face for a kiss. The thought shocked her.

Shaking away the pleasant image, she extended her right hand. "Hello, Pete. It's good to see you."

His grip was warm and strong, and he held her hand far longer than was necessary. "Hungry?" he asked finally.

"Yes, it's been a long day."

He nodded and slipped a big hand under her elbow. "Then let's go. You know what I've been hankering for?"

"No. What?"

"Another of those burned-to-a-crisp steaks." He slid his hand down from her elbow and captured hers.

It was good to hold her hand again, good to touch her. He would have liked to pull her into his arms, feel her close against him. He'd wanted to do it that other time, as well. But after his wife... He told himself to forget about Annie—this was someone else.

He watched Hope climb into the truck and smooth the blue denim of her skirt. She wasn't nearly as relaxed as she'd been before. He thought about that as he started out the lane.

He'd watched her the last few weeks, out there in the arena. She was a cool one when she faced the bulls down. Even Old Devil Eyes, who'd put more than one bullrider in the hospital, didn't seem to faze her.

But he was having second thoughts about having hired her. And third and fourth thoughts, for that matter. After all, the work *was* dangerous. A bull could kill. That was why the clown was there in the first place, to keep the downed riders from being stomped or gored. But, hell, life was dangerous no matter how you looked at it. At least in the arena she knew what she was facing.

No, it was the other danger that bothered him more. The danger to him. Somehow she'd worked herself into his blood. He could hardly keep his eyes off her, even in that ridiculous clown getup.

When he'd left her that night at her ranch he'd known he shouldn't go back. He'd just said he would call, not that he would see her again. It wasn't that he didn't want to see her again. But she was too good to be true, this little bit of a woman. And he'd been hurt so much already. He couldn't take any more hurt. He wouldn't.

But he couldn't stop thinking about her, couldn't stop remembering the brightness of her eyes, the softness of her smile, the warmth of her voice. So finally he'd decided the best way to get her out of his system was to see her again. Face-to-face he would see things he'd missed before. Face-to-face he would see that she was just a woman, like any other.

But it hadn't worked that way. Seeing her made him feel so good inside, it was almost like winning another championship buckle.

He was losing it, he told himself ruefully. Hadn't he promised himself? No more involvement with women. He might be lonely, but loneliness wasn't nearly as painful as what he'd been through before.

"Say," Hope said, interrupting his thoughts. "I've been wondering. Did you ever hire that Hobie fellow?"

Pete gave her a swift glance as he swung the truck out onto the road. She had nerve, all right. "Yeah, I took him on," he said.

Hope waited, but Pete seemed absorbed in his driving. She wondered if she'd said too much. But wasn't it logical to ask about Hobie?

"Is he working out?" she asked, turning in the seat to look at him.

Pete shrugged his broad shoulders under his tan suede jacket and shoved his dark Stetson to the back of his head. "Reckon so. He's quick on his feet, all right." He laughed. "But then he's just a little fellow. Not a big lummox like me."

"You're not a lummox!" Hope's defense was so fast that it surprised even her. "You're more like a brown bear."

"Slow and grumpy?" he said teasingly, his mouth curving in a smile.

She wanted to touch him. She wanted it bad. "No," she said. "Big and strong and—" The words stuck in her throat as he took her hand. She swallowed twice. "And friendly."

He chuckled and took his hand away. "Yeah, well, I guess I'd rather be a bear than a Brahma. Leastways I'm not mean."

Hope shivered, remembering the rage in the bull's eyes that afternoon. Sometimes the Brahmas seemed more than angry animals. Sometimes they seemed like evil incarnate. She pushed the worry away. She wouldn't let anything spoil this evening. She'd been thinking about it, hoping for it, for weeks.

Suddenly Pete pulled the pickup off the side of the road and stopped.

"What is it?" Hope asked.

"You'll see." He went around and opened her door. Taking her hand, he led her through a cattle gate.

The prairie stretched away in all directions. No buildings anywhere in sight. No other cars on this stretch of road.

A meadowlark flew off, fluttering his wings, then sailing for a while, then fluttering his wings again. For a moment Hope watched it, envying the bird its joyous flight.

Then she turned to Pete. "What is it?" she asked again. "Why did you stop here?"

He put an arm around her waist. "So we could listen."

Within the circle of his arm, Hope stood, hardly daring to breathe. She was intensely aware of the feel of him, of the nearness of him. The scent of sage was strong, there on the prairie. Mingled with it was the sweetness of the wildflowers that dotted the grass around them.

But Hope was only vaguely aware of her surroundings. Her whole being was focused on the man whose side pressed against hers, whose arm circled her shoulders. She wanted to pull his arm tighter around her, to burrow into the shelter of his chest, to raise her face for the kiss she ached to feel. But she just stood there in the prairie silence, listening.

"Isn't the silence great?" Pete asked, tightening his arm a little.

"Yes. There's nothing quite like prairie stillness."

"I love it," Pete said. "After all the racket in the arena it seems so peaceful."

They stood there for some minutes longer, a faint ticking from the truck's cooling radiator adding a quiet rhythm to the gentle hum of insects.

"Well," Pete said finally. "Guess we'd better get on down the road. I'm past ready to eat."

As they pulled out onto the pavement again, Hope smiled to herself. Pete Hamilton might look like any rough-and-tumble cowboy, but underneath he was a gentle, sensitive man. She liked that.

The restaurant wasn't crowded, and the waitress smiled as she took their order.

"Now," Pete said. "Tell me about your day."

For one wild moment Hope wanted to tell him about looking into the Brahma's angry eyes. She wanted to share with him the fear and the elation, the sense of being someone special. She wanted to let him see deep inside herself.

But of course she couldn't. She swallowed her disappointment. "Nothing much to tell," she said. "Just the usual bunch of chores. Drive here, drive there, get this, get that."

The lie sat heavy in her stomach, like too many doughy flapjacks from a tenderfoot cook's griddle.

"You know," she went on, picking at her salad, "there's something I'd like to ask you."

He grinned. "Anything. Ask me anything at all."

The warmth in his eyes raised an answering warmth inside her. She recognized it and was not surprised. Every glimpse of him these last weeks had made her feel good, had helped ease her aching muscles. They'd even made her better able to face the bulls.

"I'm curious about how you got into rodeo," she said. "Clint was born to it, more or less, since his father competed." She liked it that they could speak of Clint, easily, without constraint.

"Actually, I was a city boy." Pete grinned. "Born and raised in Butte. My daddy was a schoolteacher. I even know how to talk right. But talking uppity doesn't get me points with cowboys."

His grin widened. "Daddy came here from back East. He met Mama and stayed on. He didn't know much about horses, but he loved the West. Said it was like a storybook come true."

Pete whistled between his teeth. "And that man was rodeo-crazy. Still is. He catches every rodeo within a hundred miles of Houston. That's where they live now. Yeah, I grew up on rodeo. Mama says I was three months old when they took me to my first." He sipped his coffee. "And soon as I could talk that's what I talked about. Rodeo."

"When did you start competing?" Hope forgot her salad, lost in visions of a wide-eyed little boy.

"Soon as I could I got in the junior rodeo. I rode the broncs bareback, even did a little roping." He chuckled. "I wasn't too good at that. But I could stick to those broncs. Like glue."

"How many silver buckles?" Hope asked.

Pete brought his free hand automatically to his belt. "Three," he said. "I was heading for number four last time I got thrown. I broke my leg in three different places and banged up my knee." He paused, his coffee cup halfway to his mouth. "I was raring to go, though, soon as the doc gave the word."

Hope saw the pain in his eyes before he could mask it. Pain and disappointment. Like most rodeo cowboys, he'd found competition awfully hard to give up.

"But the doc said it was time to quit—if I wanted to keep on riding and walking, that is. And I did."

"That must have been hard." She wanted him to know she understood.

He nodded. "Yeah, but you know what they say: 'There's never a horse that couldn't be rode, and there's never a rider that couldn't be throwed.' Clint and I used to talk about competing when he rode the bulls. Before he took to clowning."

His grin seemed to envelop her in a special warmth. "He said his wife got him out of riding. But since bulls were in his blood he talked her into letting him clown."

Hope nodded and swallowed uncomfortably. This was getting too close to home. "Did your wife object to your bronc-riding?" She wished the words back as soon as she'd said them. A closed, strange look came over his face. He looked like someone else, a complete stranger. But he answered.

"Naw, she liked it," he said. "She always was a woman for excitement. I met her at a rodeo down Augusta way. I had two silvers then."

Pete cut off a bite of the steak the waitress had just put in front of him and nodded his approval. "Exactly right," he said. Thank goodness the waitress had come then. He didn't like talking about Annie. He never had and never would.

For a few minutes the two of them were busy eating. Then Hope asked, "How old were you when you quit?"

"Pushing twenty-five." He managed a smile. "Almost ten years now. I had some money saved." He grinned a little. "Not that I didn't do my share of whooping it up. I did, for sure. But my daddy had a real thing about saving. He got me started putting part of every purse in the bank. And when the doc said get out or else, I had a good little nest egg to do it with."

He broke a piece of bread in half. "I thought about clowning. But I'm too big a man, not fast enough on my feet. So I got into the promoting end of things. And I do some announcing now and then."

He wondered what she was thinking. Her eyes were so big, so intent. Was she thinking about Clint? About their life together? Or about the bulls she faced in the arena? Or was she laughing to herself at the big dumb cowboy she'd been fooling?

No, he told himself. She's not laughing. Not Hope.

He buttered the bread slowly, evenly. "Don't know if you've ever noticed, but most rodeo cowboys aren't real big. Five-nine maybe. All that wrenching around isn't good for a man's spine. And, like the doc said, the longer your spine is, the more you've got to mess up."

He saw her catch her breath, saw her pause, a forkful of steak halfway to her mouth. He could tell from her eyes that she knew. She knew there was nothing more terrifying to a cowboy than the thought of being unable to get on a horse. His stomach clenched at the thought, at the remembered fear.

Her eyes were intent on him. Wide brown eyes filled with concern. "You didn't—"

"Naw," he told her. "Doc said it'd be fine if I stayed off the broncs."

They turned their attention to their dinners then, but as she ate, Hope's mind was alive with images. A younger, lighter Pete with spurs flying along a bucking bronc's flanks. She could see the look of triumph when he made a good score, the disgust when he got dumped. She even saw him surrounded by giggling rodeo groupies, his silver buckle shining.

They lingered at the table, talking, sipping coffee. It was late when Pete turned the truck toward the Circle C again. As he drove through the cattle gate and up the lane to the darkened house, Hope swallowed a sigh. Their long-awaited evening was over, and she didn't want it to end. She wanted . . .

Pete took her hand and walked beside her up the moonlit path to the porch. "Thank you for dinner," she said as they stopped in front of the door. "I really enjoyed it." She turned toward him. He was very close. Again she caught the good scent of horses, leather and sage.

In the shadows his face was dark and mysterious, but there was no mistaking the warmth in his eyes. "I'm the one should be thanking you," he said, his voice husky. "I haven't felt this good in years."

Those bright blue eyes burned into hers, heating her whole body.

Maybe it was the way she returned his look, or maybe it was the way she lifted her chin. Anyway, he didn't bother with words. He just gathered her against his big chest, lifting her boots clean off the floor, and kissed her soundly.

Hope had half expected his kiss, had wanted it. But still the force of it took her by surprise. This wasn't the gentle kiss of acquaintance she might have expected. This was the kiss of a man who could scarcely contain his longing, his passion. This was the kiss of a man who wanted, who needed. It raised an answering need deep within her and, wrapping her arms around his neck, she returned it.

When he set her back on her feet, her legs would hardly hold her up. She clung to him for support.

"Hope—"

She put a silencing finger to his lips. "Ssh."

She thought he might kiss her again. She hoped he would. But he looked stunned, like a downed rider who'd hit the dirt too hard.

"I gotta go," he said finally, his lips against her ear. They brushed her forehead, her cheek, grazed her mouth in a fleeting caress.

He put her away from him and started for the steps. "'Bye now."

Hope's heart seemed to pause, but then it finally began beating again. She couldn't believe it. He'd said nothing about seeing her again, nothing about calling her.

She stood watching until the wagon's taillights had disappeared into the darkness.

Chapter Four

The next Thursday, Hope stood behind the chutes at Red Lodge, waiting for the bullriding to begin. She listened as the crowd responded to Pete's talk about the performers and the animals. He played the crowds the way she played the bulls. Leading them this way and that. But the crowd was easier to control.

Ordinarily she enjoyed listening to Pete's spiel, but today she was conscious only of the sound of his voice, not of his words. Over and over in the last few days she'd remembered him saying, "'Bye now," in that strange, choked way. Over and over she had tried to figure out what had happened. One minute she'd been kissing him and the next she'd been watching his taillights disappear down the lane. She still remembered feeling as if the bottom had dropped out of her stomach—and her life.

For the hundredth time she wished she knew more about Pete's wife. She only remembered that the woman was gone. Clint had never been one to gossip. He had told her more stories about the bulls he'd fought than about the men he'd traveled with. And Pete had been working one of the other circuits when she'd traveled with Clint.

The crowd roared at something else Pete had said. Hope hitched up her baggy pants and leaned her arms against the railing.

Charlie Rivers came up from behind her. "Evening, Hobie."

"Hi, Charlie." Hope smiled. The young cowboy always reminded her of Matt.

"That Pete's got a way with people," Charlie observed, leaning against the railing beside her.

"Yeah," Hope said. "He makes them laugh, all right." For a moment she and Charlie watched the action in the arena. Then she swallowed. "Guess he's real popular. Some woman was asking about him the other day. Wanted to know if he was married."

She gnawed at her lower lip, hardly able to believe she'd done such a thing. How could she have said that? She surely didn't want it to get back to Pete that Hobie was asking questions about his personal life.

Charlie shook his head. He didn't seem to see anything strange in their talk. "Pete was married once. A real mistake."

Hope tried to keep her voice level. "Oh?" She would *not* ask any more leading questions. She held her breath, waiting for him to go on. "How so?"

Charlie frowned. "Annie Smithers was as wild as they come. Couldn't no man tame her." He sighed. "We all felt for Pete. He was real broke up when she got killed."

Hope was silent. Now she understood the hurt he must have gone through.

Charlie straightened. "Well, guess I'd better go get my rig ready. I'm up soon. Got to make that day money."

Hope nodded. "See you later." So Pete's wife had been wild. Whatever that meant.

But surely that wasn't the reason for Pete's behavior the other night. Surely he didn't think *she* was like Annie.

"And now, ladies and gents..." His words intruded into her thoughts, bringing her to full alertness. "Our bullriders'll be showing their stuff. We've got some of the rankest bulls in the whole West here today. And some of the best bullriders this state has ever seen." The crowd applauded.

"And one of the best clowns, too. Our own Hobie Brown."

That was her cue. Hope pranced into the arena, waving her huge orange hankie to the crowd and bowing to right and left.

"First up," Pete continued, "is Charlie Rivers of Butte on a bull named Bread Basket. Charlie's been having himself a real good season."

Charlie would be glad to be up first, Hope thought. He didn't like waiting. She was always tense herself. It never failed to amaze her the way eight seconds could seem like a lifetime. When a rider was up on a bull, time faded into slow motion.

But when the rider was down, time speeded up. Then there weren't even seconds for thinking, for working through what to do. Then it was all reaction. Knowledge of the best moves had to be there, in her mind, but it was instinct that told her body what to do. Instinct and the training Clint had drilled into her.

The qualifying buzzer sounded, and Charlie let go of his rope. But just as his boots hit the ground the bull twisted, whacking the cowboy with his shoulder and sending him flying. He hit the sawdust hard.

Hope was there the next second, dancing in front of the angry bull, luring him away until Charlie could regain his breath. She swallowed a sigh of relief as he scrambled to safety and the bull trotted off toward the open gate.

The bullriding events went by quickly—all too quickly for Hope. When they were over she was free again to let her mind dwell on Pete Hamilton. And that didn't do her any good at all.

She turned away from the arena, her thoughts in turmoil. Part of her wanted to march right up to Pete and demand an explanation. Why had he left her like that? Why hadn't he called her since?

She couldn't do that, of course. Even if she could have done it without giving away her secret, she'd never been one to chase after men. Approaching Clint that day in Glasgow had taken all the guts she'd had. Besides, how could you ask a man why he didn't want to see you again? It was degrading, humiliating....

She shook her head. She had to stop this. It wasn't getting her anywhere. Her nerves were shot. And she couldn't afford that in her line of work.

Taking a good deep breath, she pulled in the comforting odor of horses and leather. Mixed with them came the smell of popcorn and deep-fried food. Her stomach rumbled, reminding her that it had been a long time since she'd eaten anything. Maybe she'd better—

The hand that came down on her shoulder took her breath away and stopped her in her tracks. "Hold it there, Hobie," Pete said. The touch of his hand made her bones want to melt. All the anger and hurt she'd been feeling toward him disappeared, all because of one little touch.

Her heart leapt up in her throat and did a wild dance of joy. And then it fell, ricocheting off the bottom of her stomach, as she started wondering what it was he wanted from her.

She moistened her lips. "Hi, boss. What do you want?"

She had stopped, but she didn't turn to look up into his eyes. Pete cursed himself silently. His hand was still on her shoulder. He knew he should move it. But Lord, how soft and warm that shoulder felt.

He fought the temptation to yank her into his arms and crush her against him. He wanted to kiss her so badly it hurt. He would look like a damn fool, too, he told himself. Kissing the rodeo clown! You would never be able to live that one down.

"You've been doing a great job, Hobie," he said, feeling like a fool anyway. "Keep it up."

There was a moment's silence. "Thanks, boss. I will."

She was so cool, so collected. Suddenly he wanted to rile her a little. "Say, Hobie, why don't we have a bite together? Get to know each other?" Under his fingers he could feel the tenseness building in her shoulder.

She still didn't look at him. How was she going to get out of this? This time he cursed his own contrariness. Why did they have to play these silly games? Why couldn't they just be themselves?

Then she spoke. "Gee, boss," she said, "I'd really like to. But I been having some trouble."

"Trouble?" What kind of trouble was she going to invent? Or was it real? His stomach churned. Something wrong at the ranch? Something with her health?

"Yeah," she said. "It's . . . well, I got this drinking problem. I got to go to a meeting tonight. You know— AA. But thanks, anyway."

For another long moment he stood there, trying to think of something to say, something that wouldn't sound stupid. "Well," he said finally, "keep up the good work."

"I will, boss," she said.

And then she was gone, slipping out from under his hand. Gone without ever having looked him in the face. He stood there for a moment, his heart racing. That AA excuse . . . Did she know about Annie?

He turned and slowly retraced his steps to the office. So what if she did? He hadn't done anything to be ashamed of. Except . . . He pushed the old feelings of helplessness down. Annie's drinking had been *her* problem. He'd recognized that long ago.

He shoved his hands deep into his pockets. What a dumb thing to do, putting Hope on the spot like that. He'd given her the job because he'd wanted to help the woman, not play games with her. Her deceiving him rankled, though. Why couldn't she have come to him straight out? Told him the truth?

But then he wasn't sure *he* would have hired her, either. Maybe he'd have been like the others. Maybe he'd have seen only a delicate-looking woman instead of a well-trained clown. Maybe he would have made the same mistake.

Well, at least she was good at talking herself out of trouble. Almost as good as Annie. But then, weren't women always good at lying?

He winced at the cruel thought. He knew he ought to stay away from Clint's widow. But Lord, the woman pulled at him. She drew him the way green spring grass drew his winter-weary steers.

With a frown, he strode into the office and slammed the door behind him.

Hope stood for a moment in her motel room, her body trembling at the remembered feel of Pete's hand on her shoulder. It no longer seemed strange to her that she should respond to him.

She'd loved Clint, but he was gone. And now she was drawn to Pete. How much she wanted to have dinner with him, to recapture the joy of the other night. There was no way she could do that as Hobie Brown.

Pulling off the wig, she tossed it on the bed. The garish clown face stared back at her from the mirror. This thing wasn't such a good idea. Her feelings for Pete were too strong. She was going to get hurt.

But what could she do? The ranch needed the money from her work. And, she admitted to herself, she needed to be around Pete, even if it was only as Hobie Brown.

As she scrubbed off her makeup and the grime of the arena, she went over what had just happened. Thank goodness she knew enough about AA from Clint's dad to have come up with that excuse. Before his death he'd spoken quite freely to his family about the AA program and how it had helped him.

Hope finished showering and toweled herself dry. If only she could have gotten this job some other way. If only she could have met Pete some other way. She sighed. If-onlys never helped anyone.

The rest of the evening stretched ahead of her. She would have to decide between peanut butter and jelly and going out to look for some inconspicuous place to eat.

Room service was far too expensive to use. As it was, she stayed at the cheapest motels. And if she worked a one-day show and it wasn't too far away, she didn't even get a room. She just drove back and forth and changed in some gas station.

She piled up pillows against the headboard of the bed, then opened the makeup case that Claire had stocked with food for her. What she would really like, Hope thought as she spread peanut butter and jelly on crackers, was a nice juicy steak. And Pete Hamilton's company.

But she knew it was dangerous to go out. Red Lodge wasn't such a big town. Actually, most of the towns on the circuit weren't very big. Montana wasn't exactly a state of big cities.

If she went out she might easily run into Pete. It wasn't that she didn't want to see him, but if she did she'd have to lie even more.

Hope sighed. She wasn't good at this sort of thing. Clint had always said her eyes gave her away. It all came back to the ranch. It was all Matt had left of his father, and if it hadn't been at stake she would have told Pete the truth.

She sighed and brushed cracker crumbs off the front of her robe. There didn't seem to be any good way out of this. It looked as if she would just have to tough it out. After all, it was only until September. And the way it looked—after the other night—she and Pete might not be getting together again.

Half an hour later she tossed aside the mystery novel Claire had thoughtfully included. She simply couldn't concentrate on anything.

She sighed again. She hadn't told Claire about what had happened with Pete that night. It seemed almost silly to feel such terrible loss because he hadn't called again. They'd only been out together twice.

After all, Pete hadn't promised her anything. Just because his kiss had made her come alive again, made her feel like a woman once more...that didn't have to mean *he* was feeling so much.

A man like Pete, a man with his lean good looks and friendly, good-natured personality, could have any woman he wanted.

Hope frowned. That wife of his must have been crazy. Imagine not appreciating a man like that.

She turned off the lamp and slid down in the bed. She was spending too much time speculating about Pete Hamilton. Maybe he just wanted time to think. Or maybe he was flustered. Or...

She flopped over on her side. There were a million maybes, and she would never know which one was the reason for Pete's behavior. She'd better just forget about him and go to sleep.

The arena looked fuzzy. The faces of the crowd, even of the cowboys perched on the railing, had a strange, hazy look to them. But the bull in front of her was in sharp focus, from its wet nostrils to its coarse hair. He loomed as big as a two-story building, yet his eyes were level with her own. They were vicious eyes, gleaming with hatred.

The bull snorted, nostrils flaring, and pawed the earth with a hoof the size of a bulldozer.

Hope's breath seemed caught in her throat. And the commands she gave her body were suspended somewhere between her brain and the limbs she was sending them to. She told her arms to wave, but they hung heavy at her sides. She told her feet to move, but they were lead, impossible to drag.

She stood there, utterly paralyzed, so close that the bull's fetid breath threatened to suffocate her.

The bull shook his huge head from side to side, tossing its wickedly gleaming horns. His eyes held her fast, keeping her prisoner. She read evil in those eyes. Evil and hatred. And death.

And then he charged.

Her scream rent the darkness of the motel room. Trembling, she sat bolt upright in the strange bed, clutching the covers to her clammy flesh.

Her breath was coming in great gasps, and she reached for the light switch. In the light the unfamiliar room took on a sane, everyday look. "It was just a dream," she told herself, willing her body to relax, willing herself to calm down and breathe evenly. "And a stupid one at that. Who ever heard of a bull that big?"

But somehow the words weren't that comforting. The evil of the bull had been so clear. His hatred had seemed almost personal, as though it were her—and her alone—that he was out to get.

As her pounding heart slowed, Hope frowned and reached for the mystery again. "Next time," she told herself, "I'm bringing something dull and boring to read. Something that will put me to sleep in a hurry."

She finally managed to get to sleep again—but not, unfortunately, until she'd read the entire novel. So the next morning she was not at her best. Her muscles complained as though she'd really been fighting that dream bull. Her mind felt hazy and cloudy. And on top of that she simply couldn't stand the idea of spending the time till the evening show cooped up in a motel room with her thoughts. She had to get out of there.

She dressed quickly, brushing out her long, dark hair and tying it back with a ribbon. She pulled on worn jeans and a blue plaid shirt, fished her boots out from under the bed and fetched her Stetson from the closet. "I'm going out," she said aloud. "And if I happen to run into Pete Hamilton, why, I'm just here on ranch business. Surely there's nothing wrong with that."

It wasn't the soundest excuse, but it would do. Probably she wouldn't see Pete. And even if she did, who knew if he would bother to speak to her? After the other night it was hard to know *what* the man would do.

She grabbed her purse and her jacket and locked the door behind her. Now, where was the nearest place to shop?

Chapter Five

Hope sank into the booth with a sigh of relief. Shopping hadn't been as much fun as she'd thought. It was good just to sit down, not to have to rush to do something. At least there was plenty of time for a substantial lunch. Then she wouldn't need to eat again until after the evening performance. She'd learned the hard way that food lay too heavily on her stomach if she put it there right before going into the arena.

Maybe after lunch she would wander around downtown Red Lodge. It had been a while since she'd been down to look at the old buildings in the commercial historic district. She let her mind wandor off to the old days, when men were men and women...

She could see herself, in a long homespun dress, waiting by the door of their sod hut. And Pete striding across the prairie toward her. They might have built a home on that very meadow where they'd stopped to listen to the silence. She let herself imagine that he had reached the door, that he'd taken her into his arms. They were strong arms, the arms of a man who loved her—

"Hope? Hope Crenshaw!"

Pete's voice jerked her out of her reverie. She looked up to see him grinning down at her like some kind of miracle.

"What're you doing so far from home?" He slid into the seat across from her.

She pulled herself together, back into reality, and reached for the answer she'd rehearsed. "Oh, just some ranch business. You know how it is."

It was good to be able to look right at him, right into his eyes. As Hobie she never allowed herself that privilege. But she didn't want to let too much of her happiness show. After all, this was the man who'd walked away from her. Even after kissing her the way he had.

Now he was smiling at her, just as if everything was fine between them. Just as if—

"Maybe you'll have time to see the show while you're here." He reached into his pocket. "I'll give you a free pass."

She managed not to let her feelings show on her face. "Sorry. I'd like to, but I've got a business appointment this evening."

He frowned, his dark brows drawing together. "You aren't planning on starting for home tonight?"

"No, no, I'm not."

His face grew even darker.

She wondered what he was thinking. About the way he'd left her that night on the porch? But why would that make him scowl? He was the one who'd driven away. He was the one who hadn't called.

He cleared his throat. "Maybe you'd care to have a bite to eat, then. After the show. If you're back in time, that is."

"Yes," Hope said, her heart threatening to choke her. "That sounds good."

He got to his feet. "Where're you staying? I'll call you when I get back to my room."

Hope's mind raced. She couldn't use the excuse of not having a room yet. Not on a Fourth of July weekend with the rodeo in town. Thank goodness she'd decided to register under her own name. "I'm at the Lupine Inn," she said.

Pete grinned. "I'm staying there, too. See you later."

As she watched him walk away with that peculiar cowboy stride, she knew she was grinning, too. You're an idiot, she told herself. Seeing him later was surely asking for trouble.

But nothing could dim her happiness. She floated through the rest of the afternoon like a teenager. And when she arrived at the arena she found she was still wearing a silly smile.

Even with her makeup on, young Charlie Rivers noticed it. "You're looking happier than a bullrider with a new silver buckle," he commented. "Something real nice must have happened to you."

Hope nodded, snapping her red suspenders. "Yeah," she said. "I'm feeling pretty good tonight."

Charlie frowned. "Tell you what'd make me feel good. Not drawing Old Devil Eyes. That critter's got the meanest eyes. Makes me feel like it's me special he's after."

Hope nodded. "I know what you mean. I don't like him, either. Other bulls are mean. He's—"

"Downright evil," Charlie said. "Wouldn't surprise me none if he turned into old Satan right there before my eyes."

Hope chuckled. "That'd pull in the crowd, wouldn't it?"

Charlie's smile looked a little sickly. "Yeah, guess so. Well, I just have to take the luck of the draw. And he does give a man a good ride."

Hope nodded. "Yeah. Well, take it easy."

She frowned as Charlie turned away. Cowboys, as a rule, weren't any more superstitious than ordinary folk. But if Charlie felt the bull was unlucky...

The mind was a funny thing. Charlie's beliefs could make a difference in his ability to ride.

Then she forgot about Charlie for a while. She had to. The bulls were particularly difficult today and needed all her attention. Probably they didn't like the popping of firecrackers any more than she did. She knew it was practically impossible to catch the kids who were throwing them.

There were just too many people, and the rodeo officials couldn't be everywhere. But what was wrong with parents that they hadn't taught their kids any better than that? With a pang she thought of Matt, always moving farther and farther away from her.

But she couldn't think about that, either. Each and every bull seemed on his worst behavior. She had to be on her toes every single second.

And then the announcer said, "And our last bull-rider, folks, is Charlie Rivers. Charlie hails from Butte. And he's riding Old Devil Eyes, and I know I don't have to tell you how mean that bull is."

Hope pulled in a deep breath. You can do it, Charlie, she said silently. Don't let the fear get to you.

The bull came bounding out of the chute, jerking Charlie from right to left. Hope's heart seemed to stand still. It looked as if the bull's first bound had thrown Charlie off balance, and he hadn't been able to regain it. He wasn't going to last the eight seconds. Soon now—

And then it happened. Some fool kid threw a string of firecrackers right down into the arena. The crackers landed under the bull's nose. If he'd been mad before, that made him plain crazy. First he whirled one way, then the other, in a mind-boggling display of frenzy.

When he switched directions, Charlie lost his precarious balance and flew off. He landed right by the still-exploding crackers.

Damn! Hope put her body between the bull and the fallen man. The bull's eyes were glazed. He swung his huge horns and pawed the sawdust.

"No!" Hope didn't know whether she yelled it aloud or just thought it. "You're not getting him," she said. "Not while I'm here."

The bull shook his head again. The great folds of skin under his neck swung back and forth, menacing in their heaviness. For a second she wondered if he could really understand her. If he really wanted to destroy people. Then she stopped herself. That kind of thinking didn't help at all.

"Get!" she yelled. "Get out of here."

Behind her, the firecrackers had finished exploding. In front of her, the bull waited. For another long moment he stared at her. Then he turned and trotted out the gate.

The crowd roared its appreciation, but Hope hurried to where Charlie lay. His cheek was blackened where one of the crackers had whipped around and caught him. One leg was bent at a funny angle. It was broken, Hope thought. Broken, for sure.

Charlie groaned. "I can't see. Oh, God, I can't see."

He sounded like Matt when he'd been hurt. Without thinking, Hope reached for his hand. "Hold on, Charlie," she said. "We'll get you to the doctors."

The hand she had picked up enclosed hers in a fierce grip. "My wife," Charlie said.

"We'll call her."

"No, don't!" His hand clung to hers. "She's expecting. Only five weeks to go. And the doc said no excitement and no traveling. It's our third try. Gotta make it this time."

"Okay, Charlie." Hope soothed him as she would have Matt. "It's okay. What about your mother? Where can I call her?"

"She's gone," he said. "Pop, too."

Her heart contracted as she remembered her own pain.

"Do you have a buddy here?" she asked. "Someone to go to the hospital with you?"

Charlie shook his head. "No. Rich didn't come along this trip. His favorite mare's foaling along about now. Hobie?" His grip tightened. "Hobie, would you come with me?"

"Sure." There was no other answer she could give. If it had only been something broken, Charlie wouldn't even have asked. He'd have been joking with the pickup men in spite of his pain. But to be blinded . . . Her stomach twisted with the fear of it.

The ambulance men had Charlie, still clinging to her hand, on the stretcher before she remembered she was supposed to meet Pete. Settling beside Charlie in the ambulance, she told herself she would come up with some excuse. Later.

An hour and a half later, leaning wearily against the waiting room wall, she ran over the possibilities for the hundredth time. Anything to keep her mind occupied through the endless waiting. If only they would come and tell her about Charlie.

She thought about his young wife, trying so hard to bring a new life into the world. And Charlie, out there risking his neck, giving the bull a chance to take him out of it.

She had insisted that Clint give up riding the bulls. But that hadn't saved him. Life was risky all around. There were no guarantees.

The best thing, it seemed, the only sensible thing, was to just love as much as you could while you could. At least that way you would have fewer regrets. Like her and Clint.

She closed her eyes. She was so tired. Tired of waiting, tired of pretending, tired—

"Hobie. I came as quick as I could."

The voice woke her from a pleasant dream. A man had been there, in the dream, a man she loved.

"Pete?" For a moment she couldn't think. He was still part of the dream. And then she came awake, remembering where she was. Who she was. "Hello, boss."

He folded himself into the chair beside her. "How's Charlie?"

She shook her head. "I don't know. They're still working on him. He—he said he couldn't see. Those kids and their firecrackers."

Pete patted her shoulder roughly. He wanted to take her in his arms, to hold her and comfort her, but of course he couldn't.

Lord, she looked like hell. Even under the clown makeup he could see her exhaustion. "Where's his wife?" he asked. "She ought to be here."

Hope stared down at her baggy pants. "She's expecting. He said not to call her."

"She ought to be here," Pete repeated. "Time like this, a man needs his woman." For a moment *he* was lying in a hospital bed, a leg in traction, an arm in a cast, with taped ribs and a split lip. And wondering where Annie was, why she didn't come to him.

For a second he felt the pain again, like a kick in the gut.

Hope shook her head. "She's miscarried twice, Charlie said. He doesn't want to bring this delivery on too soon."

Pete sighed. Other people's love seemed strange to him, a kind of magic he couldn't understand. "Guess we'd better do what he says, then."

She turned to face him. Evidently her concern for Charlie overrode her fear of looking him in the face. "What do you think, boss? About his eyes?"

He heard the terror and knew some of it was Charlie's. How could a blind man ride? And if he couldn't ride, how could he work?

"Don't know," he said. "Seems like maybe if it was just from the crackers they could get better. But if he hit his head and it's something else—"

"I don't think so. Seems to me his shoulder hit and then his leg bent under him."

He wanted to give her all the comfort he could. Lord, how he longed to touch her. "Then maybe his sight'll come back. I guess—"

The doctor came through the swinging doors, and she was on her feet instantly. Without thinking, he put out a hand to steady her. She didn't even notice.

"How is he?"

"Mr. Rivers is resting comfortably."

"His eyes. What about his eyes?"

The doctor shook his head. "There appears to have been some corneal abrasion. We can't tell if the damage is irreversible. It's like any other scrape. We have to wait to see if it heals."

He frowned. "We've put him in a room, but he says he has to talk to some Hobie before we sedate him."

"That's me."

"I'm coming, too." Pete wasn't going to let her go in there alone. She looked as if she might keel over any minute.

The doctor nodded. "Room 305."

They were there in minutes.

"Charlie." Hope rushed to the bedside.

"Hi, Hobie. Thanks for waiting. You've been a real pal."

"Pete's here," Hope said. "He came to see how you're doing."

For a moment Charlie's face twisted, the part she could see under the bandages. "Doing okay," he said. "If I could only see."

"You'll be fine," Hope said, praying it was true. "The doctor says it'll just take time."

"Time." Charlie's voice rose. "What time is it getting to be?"

"Around eleven," Pete said.

Charlie looked relieved. "Listen, Hobie, will you do one more thing for me?"

"Sure. What is it?"

"Dial Mary Lou for me. I talk to her every night around this time."

"Are you sure—?"

"I can talk," Charlie said. "I'll tell her about my leg. No need to mention the eyes. Till we know for sure, that is."

Hope hesitated. Surely Charlie's wife had a right to the truth. But she could see his side of it, too. There was the baby to think of.

She looked at Pete. His face was set in dark lines. "What do you think, boss?" she asked.

Pete shrugged. "It's not up to us to tell her the truth. Charlie's got to decide that. But for myself I think the truth's always best."

Hope looked at the man in the bed. "Guess I agree with Pete," she said. "People deserve the truth." She paused, thinking of the big man standing beside her. Wishing she could... "But sometimes we're afraid to give it to them."

"I'll tell her about the leg," Charlie repeated. "But I'm going to see again. No sense in worrying her about that."

There was a touch of hysteria in his voice, but Hope decided to ignore it. It couldn't hurt him to believe he was going to be all right. And it might help.

She dialed the number and handed Charlie the phone.

"Hi, honey," he said. "How you doing? Great. Me? Oh, I'm okay. Just got a little broken leg." There was a pause. "Now, honey, you promised. You just think about the baby. I'll be fine. Yeah, I got buddies here. Pete Hamilton. And that clown, Hobie, the one I told you about. He kept the bull off me."

There was another pause while he listened. "That's good, honey. Listen, I got to go to sleep. They gave me this shot. Now you stay put. Take care of our little one. I'll be home soon as I get out of here. Love you."

Hope put the receiver back in the cradle. "Now will you let them give you that shot?"

Charlie nodded. "Yeah, tell them to bring in their old needle. I can sleep now."

Outside in the corridor, Pete turned to her. "Can I give you a lift?"

Hope hesitated. At that moment she realized she had nothing with her, no money, not even a credit card. Everything was still in the wagon, parked at the arena.

She was bone-tired. It was late at night. "I'd be obliged," she said. "I'm at the Lupine Inn."

A strange expression crossed his face. What was he thinking?

"A lot of us are staying there," he said. He glanced at his watch and shook his head. "Fact is, after the show I was supposed to meet a pretty lady for a bite to eat."

"Oh?" She was too exhausted to think straight, but she knew she liked it that he'd called her pretty.

"Yeah. She probably thinks I stood her up."

Hope climbed wearily into the pickup. "If she's a lady, she'll believe you when you tell her about Charlie. And if she isn't—" She stopped. She shouldn't remind him of Annie. That wouldn't be smart.

Pete slammed his door shut. "I don't know. Wouldn't blame her if she didn't. Seems like people lie to each other all the time these days."

Hope swallowed over the lump in her throat. "Maybe they think they're doing the right thing. Like Charlie." Why did their conversation have to be so loaded? It seemed as if everything he said had a double meaning. Could he have figured out who she was? But surely if he had he would have said something to her. He had no reason to keep quiet.

Tired as she was, she was ready when they got to the motel. "Thanks for the ride," she said, jumping out of the truck. "See you."

She was already in the elevator before she realized that she really had left everything at the arena, including the key to her room. She would have to go to the desk. And if Pete was still around...

She rode the elevator to the top floor and then down again. When the doors opened, she scanned the lobby. Thank God it was empty. She hurried across to the desk.

"There was an accident at the rodeo," she told the clerk. "I went to the hospital with the injured rider. I need the key to my room—209."

"Yes, of course. Mr..."

"Crenshaw. H." Thank goodness she'd decided to make reservations with her initial.

"Yes. Here it is, Mr. Crenshaw."

She was conscious of his curious look as she hurried off, but she no longer cared. She just wanted to be in her room. Safe. And clean. And lying flat.

As she pulled the door closed behind her, the phone began ringing. She grabbed it up.

"Hello."

"Hello, Hope. It's Pete. Sorry to call so late. I got hung up."

"It's okay." She took a deep breath to steady her nerves. "I waited a while. Then I figured something had come up. So I took a shower and got ready for bed."

"Does that mean it's too late to meet me?"

Longing welled up in her, but she was so tired. Too tired to be careful about what she said. "I'm afraid so, Pete. I've got a long day tomorrow."

"How about tomorrow night?"

She really wanted to see him, but there was the long drive home, and the promise she'd made to ride with Matt. She had to honor that. "I'm sorry, Pete. I'd like to, but I've got to get back to the ranch."

There was a pause. And then, almost as though he didn't want to do it, he asked. "Well, then, what about breakfast?"

Somehow that pause decided her. "Breakfast sounds fine, Pete."

"Okay. See you in the dining room at eight sharp. Good night."

"Good night." Hope put the receiver back on the hook and headed for the shower. She might as well admit it. Pete Hamilton was meaning more and more to her. And she didn't know what she was going to do about it.

Chapter Six

Good morning." Hope slid into the booth across from Pete.

"Morning."

He didn't look so good. His eyes were cloudy and his face was drawn. Actually, she hadn't slept much herself. Every time she'd drifted off she'd heard Charlie's frightened voice exclaiming that he couldn't see.

"You look tired," she said, picking up the menu.

"Yeah. I didn't sleep too good. One of our bull-riders is in the hospital." He frowned. "He's just a kid, really. And now he can't see."

"No wonder you're worried." She tried to remain calm. It was sort of like fighting a bull, being across the table from Pete. She had to watch every step. In either case, she had a lot to lose and the stakes were equally high. "Tell me what happened."

Pete told her. "...and so," he finished, "the doctors say we'll just have to wait."

"I'm sorry." She wanted to do something to ease his pain.

He shrugged, and his frown deepened. "The worst of it is, the kid's got no one else. And I can't hang around to be there for him. I've got a commitment down in Houston. A big one."

"Do you want me to stay?" The words were out before she thought. "I could make arrangements to stay for a couple days longer."

"Would you?" He seemed relieved. Some of the strain left his face. "The kid's so young. And with his wife not coming—"

"Don't worry about him. I'll stay." Matt was going to be upset, but surely she could make him understand. Their all-day ride could wait a day or two.

She and Pete talked about other, everyday things while they ate. She felt a sweet contentment just being with him.

But when he'd finished his coffee he said, "I'm leaving right after the show this afternoon. Meet me at the hospital and I'll introduce you to Charlie."

"I...I..." For the first time she realized the implications of what she'd promised. But she couldn't think of a way out. "Okay," she replied, angling for time.

Pete got to his feet. He covered her hand with his briefly, making her want to clutch it and tell him the truth. But she didn't. She couldn't.

"Thanks," he said. And then he was gone.

Hope stared into her coffee cup. How was she going to get out of this one?

She would have to call Matt and explain why their ride was canceled. That wasn't going to be easy. He'd been acting so funny lately.

And then there was the show to do. Hobie the clown still had to look out for the bullriders.

But none of that told her how she was going to handle Pete at the hospital.

And she was no closer to an answer when she arrived there after the show. She thought about letting Charlie in on her secret and asking him to keep quiet about it. But he was sure to act differently toward her if he knew.

Besides, after all that talk about truth, it was hard to say what he might think—or do. And on top of everything she couldn't even be sure she would get there before Pete did. She would just have to play it by ear.

The room was empty except for the man in the bed. He looked smaller somehow, even with his leg in the cast and bandages over his eyes. "Hi, Charlie."

"Hobie! I knew you'd come by. I felt it," Charlie said happily.

Why was it so hard to see a man like this? Hope wondered sadly. He seemed like a little boy. Probably felt like one, too, helpless as he was.

"Yeah," she said. "I thought I'd see how you're doing." She pulled up a chair.

"I'm doing okay." Charlie frowned. "Except for my eyes. But they'll be okay, too. You'll see."

Hope winced. Charlie was trusting in a man, a rodeo buddy. How would he feel if he knew who she really was? She wanted to tell him the truth about herself.

It had to be done. And she would do it. She swallowed twice. "Charlie," she began. "Do you remember Clint Crenshaw? I—"

"So, how's the best bullrider in Montana doing this morning?"

Sunshine seemed to arrive in the room with Pete. His white Stetson gleamed in his hands, and his golden-yellow shirt made her think of wild daisies in a prairie meadow. Her heart danced around in her chest until she thought she'd have to hold it down.

"Doing okay," Charlie said. "But I sure don't feel like the best bullrider anywhere. I feel like a damn fool."

"You couldn't help the firecrackers," Hope said. "It wasn't your fault."

"Yeah," Charlie said. "Ho—"

Hope's heart threatened to choke her, but she managed to cut him off in time. "Charlie and I were just talking about Clint Crenshaw," she said. "Listen, Charlie, there's something I need to talk to Pete about. We'll be right back."

"Sure."

The young cowboy looked puzzled, but at least he agreed. And thank goodness he didn't start to call her Hobie again.

Pete followed her out into the hall. He hadn't deliberately trapped her into coming to the hospital, but some little part of him was enjoying her discomfort. She thought she was so smart—fooling him. And all the time he knew who she was. And exactly what she was doing.

He took a closer look at her as she chose a seat in the waiting room. It was good to see her in female clothes, without the baggy pants and the face paint. But she was looking tired. She hadn't looked so chipper at breakfast, and she looked even more worn now, after a day's work.

"What is it?" he asked. "What'd you want to talk about?" He wanted to take her in his arms, to tell her to give up this fool business of facing crazy bulls. Surely that was the right thing to do. He would just tell her that he knew she was Hobie and he wasn't going to let her go into the arena anymore.

Suddenly he saw Annie, her dark eyes red with weeping. "Who made you God Almighty?" she asked. "Who says you know what's best for me? This is *my* life—mine. And I'll live it how I want to."

"Pete? Pete?"

He was brought back to the present by Hope's voice. No, he'd better keep his mouth shut. She knew what she was doing. And even if she didn't, she wouldn't welcome him sticking his nose into her life.

She repeated his name.

"Yes, sorry. I've got a lot on my mind. What is it?"

"I was thinking, maybe you shouldn't say anything to Charlie about me hanging around. To keep an eye on him, I mean. It might make him think things are more serious than they are."

She looked straight into his eyes. God, she was beautiful. He wanted—he pulled himself up short. Suddenly he wanted to make things easier for her. Maybe he couldn't get her out of the arena, but he didn't have to do this stupid stuff. He didn't have to make things more complicated. "Yeah. I see. You'll just sort of drop in."

"Right."

Pete nodded. "Sounds okay to me." He made himself glance at his watch. Much as he wanted to stay with her, he had to get going. "How long are you going to stay in town?" he asked.

She gnawed on her lower lip in that way she had.

"Don't know for sure," she said. "At least till Monday. Maybe by then the doctors'll know something."

Pete nodded. He reached into his pocket. "Here's my card. I'll try to get you at the motel, but if I don't reach you, you call the office. Collect. Let me know how he's doing."

"I will."

He got to his feet, and she rose, too. "Guess I'd better get going."

"Take care," she said, her voice soft, a sweet caress.

"You, too." He meant to leave it there, to just walk out. But something in her face, some yearning in her eyes, pulled at him. And the next thing he knew, right there in the waiting room, he was taking her in his arms.

She was such a little thing that he had to lift her off her feet to reach her mouth. But she hardly weighed an ounce. She brought her arms around his neck where they belonged. They felt good there.

So did her lips, soft and warm under his. And her slim body, pressed against his own, raised feelings he'd been trying hard to forget.

Fire raced through him, desire of such intensity that it was frightening. Her lips parted under his, inviting him to further intimacy.

His mind kept shouting, "Stop! This is crazy." But his body was hell-bent on claiming her, on knowing the joy her kiss promised.

Finally his mind won. In a brief instant of sanity he set her back on her feet. "I'll call you," he said, his voice gruff from the yearning that was eating him up. Then he turned and hurried away, not daring to look back.

Hope sank slowly into a chair. She would never understand the man. One minute he was all briskness and business, and the next . . . Her fingers stole to her lips. Why did he kiss her that way? As if the world might end suddenly and that moment was all they had?

She closed her eyes. She could still feel his arms around her, his body pressed against her own

"Oh, Pete," she whispered. "I wish you didn't have to go."

But wishing wasn't going to help. So she went to the ladies' room to repair her lipstick and tuck in her blouse.

"Hobie?" Charlie said as she went back into his room. "Is that you?"

"Yeah, Charlie."

Charlie's face relaxed. "Pete with you, too?"

Hope sat down. "No. He had to go. Said for you to take care."

Charlie nodded. "Pete's a good guy." He grinned. "Say, you remember when that woman asked you about Pete—whether he was married?"

Hope swallowed, conscious that she was blushing. "Yeah, I remember."

"Well, listen to this. I heard old Pete's got him a woman again! It's about time, too."

Hope's heart started that strange dance in her chest. Was that what made him act so differently? That he had a woman and he didn't know how to tell her?

She didn't want to hear what Charlie was saying anymore, but she also wanted to hear everything he knew. She had to hear.

"You have a woman?" Charlie asked.

Hope swallowed again. "Uh, no. Not now. Been on the road too much."

Charlie shook his head. "Better leave those groupies alone," he said. "They don't see anything but silver buckles."

Hope stopped herself from laughing. He was so very young—and so serious. "I ain't got a buckle," she pointed out.

Charlie frowned. "I forgot. Don't seem fair somehow. I mean, you do dangerous work. Don't seem like you get enough credit."

"Don't do it for credit," Hope said.

Charlie looked thoughtful. "Reckon not. Why *do* you do it?"

"Well—" Hope paused. "For money, I guess."

Charlie shook his head. "There's other ways to make money. Easier ways."

"Yeah. Well, I guess rodeo gets in your blood." Hope felt her way along, remembering the things Clint had said. "I like being smarter than the bulls," she said. "I like proving to myself that I can go out there, even though I'm scared."

"*You're* scared?"

"Of course," Hope said. "Only a fool wouldn't be scared. You are, aren't you?"

"Yeah." The word was so soft she hardly heard it.

"What?"

"Yeah, I'm scared. But I didn't think anybody else was."

Hope laughed. "Don't let them fool you. Every last one of them's afraid."

Charlie grinned. "Glad to hear it." His grin faded, and he brought his hand toward his bandages.

"How old are you?" Hope asked, deliberately changing the subject.

"Turned twenty last April," Charlie said. "Mary Lou's nineteen."

"And she's had two miscarriages already?"

Charlie nodded. "We been married over two years. Loved each other since we was kids." He frowned. "I sure hope she don't take it in her head to come down here. She shouldn't be traveling."

He sighed and moved restlessly in the bed. "I sure wish I could get out of here."

"I know, Charlie."

His face twisted. "It's not my leg. Hell, bones mend. And I've had lots of broken ones. But this... Hobie, a cowboy needs eyes. I gotta..." His voice trailed away.

He was so much like Matt, so young and so alone. Without thinking, Hope reached out to pat the hand that lay clenched on the sheet. A strange look crossed Charlie's face, and she drew her hand hastily back. Damnation! She would have to remember. Cowboys weren't given to friendly pats.

"Listen," Hope said. "I'll be staying till after supper. But they're not going to let me hang around after visiting hours tonight. So do you want to call Mary Lou now or wait till later?"

"You don't have to stay with me." Charlie said the words reluctantly. "I mean, I know you've got things to do."

"Yeah," Hope chuckled. "Those groupies really love my baggy pants."

Charlie laughed. Then he looked puzzled. "You know, I just realized. I've never seen you in regular clothes. I mean, without your paint and all. Why, I probably wouldn't know you."

"Probably not," Hope agreed. She wondered what he would think if he could see the *man* he thought he was talking to sitting there in a pink blouse and skirt.

"I'm not much to look at," she went on. "Not like the boss. Now there's a man." She waited, hoping Charlie would pick up on it and tell her more about Pete—and his new woman.

He nodded. "Yeah, that's why everyone's glad to hear about that woman. His wife really hurt him. Bad."

Hope tried to breathe calmly, slowly. "Yeah, you said that."

Charlie shook his head. "I heard of women drinking a lot, but Annie went too far. And the worst of it was, she blamed Pete."

Hope was almost afraid to interrupt him. "How could she blame him?"

"Said he kept trying to run her life." He frowned again. "Woman like that, she's got no business marrying."

"That's for sure. Marriage is a serious thing."

Charlie nodded again. "Now me, I done my share of heavy drinking and running around. Before we married, that is. But I don't cheat on Mary Lou. What we got's real special. Wouldn't want to spoil it."

Hope nodded, then remembered that he couldn't see her. "Yeah, when you get someone special you want to hang on to them."

Hope wished she would have a chance to do that with Pete.

"You're making me curious," she found herself saying. "This woman of Pete's . . . you heard tell what she looks like?"

"Not much," Charlie said. " 'Cepting she's a real beauty."

Hope dug her nails into her palms. Of course. A man like Pete could have anyone.

"Oh, and I heard she's got dark hair. And," Charlie continued, "she lives up Havre way. Owns a ranch, I think."

"Up Havre—" Hope's teeth clamped down hard. She almost laughed out loud. What a fool she was being. Here she was working herself into a jealous fit over some woman of Pete's, and *she* was that woman!

A wonderful feeling of relief washed over her. There was no other woman—except his dead wife.

But even thinking of Annie couldn't stop the glow that she felt at knowing Pete thought she was beautiful. He must think so, because he must have mentioned it to someone. Otherwise no one would know he'd been seeing her.

The glow kept her happy through the long evening, even through the sadness of Charlie's falsely hearty call to Mary Lou. But when she returned to the motel and called home again, the glow could not sustain her.

"He's not going to like it," Claire said when Hope told her she would be staying on a little longer at Red Lodge. "That boy's been talking about your day-long ride together ever since you left. When he gets back from Jimmy's he's going to be ticked off. Real ticked off."

"I know, Mom. But what can I do? Explain it to him."

"That's not easy, either," Claire said, "with the boy not knowing why you're away so much."

Hope gripped the receiver tightly. "You know I can't tell him. We've got to keep this quiet. Please, Mom..."

"I'll do my best, honey." Claire's voice was soothing. "I'll tell him this Charlie was a friend of his daddy. Maybe that'll help."

"Thanks."

Exhausted, Hope pulled off her clothes and climbed into bed. She hadn't counted on paying for the extra two nights. Or for the extra meals, either. Although Pete had offered to help with expenses, she'd declined as she was supposedly there on business anyway. That meant it would be a little longer before the Circle C got its new bull, before she could stop lying to Pete.

About an hour later she rolled over for the hundredth time and pounded the pillow. Tired as she was, she still couldn't sleep. Why did life have to be so full of problems? Hadn't the ranch been enough, without adding this stuff with Pete and Matt and now Charlie?

She sighed. "Life *is* problems." She could hear Clint saying that, laughing as he always had when he'd said anything serious. "Only the problems are really opportunities."

She pounded the pillow again. Some opportunity.

The phone rang, filling the room with sound. She grabbed it up. "Hello?"

"Hello, Hope. I didn't wake you, did I?"

"Pete! Hello. No. I mean, I wasn't sleeping."

"Good."

There was a pause, and she tried to collect her wits. "There's nothing new about Charlie," she said. "I spent the rest of the day there. He called his wife after supper. He still didn't tell her. She seems okay though.''

"That's good." Pete cleared his throat. "They're awfully young. Just a couple of kids, really."

"Yes," Hope said. "But I guess love doesn't care much about age."

"Guess not. How're you feeling?"

"Tired. But otherwise okay." She wished he were there. She felt a sudden need to have his arms around her, to lean against his strength. "What about you?"

"I'm lonesome," he said.

The wistfulness in his voice brought tears to her eyes and she blinked them away. "Me, too."

They talked for a while longer, about silly things of no real importance, and when he finally said goodnight she was feeling so good, so relaxed, that she fell sound asleep only minutes after she hung up the phone.

Chapter Seven

Y ou lied!'' Matt's chin was set in that stubborn way so like his father's. If she hadn't been so exasperated with him it might even have amused her.

"I didn't lie," she explained, reminding herself that *she* was the parent. "When I said I'd ride with you, I meant to do it."

"But you didn't. So you lied."

Hope rubbed her weary eyes. The drive home had been a long one. She was utterly exhausted. And now, before she could even get into the house, here was Matt behaving like a spoiled brat.

She tried another approach. "How would you like to be stuck in a hospital in a strange town? With no one around who cares about you?"

"He's got a wife. Gram said so."

Hope hung on to her patience. Barely. "His wife's going to have a baby. She can't travel. Gram told you that, too."

Matt was still glaring at her. He seemed determined not to understand. "He's got a mother."

Hope shook her head, feeling a surge of old pain. "He doesn't have a mother. She—"

Matt stamped his foot so hard the old floorboards protested. "Yeah?" he cried. "Well, I might as well not have one, either. For all the good you are."

Before she could recover from her shock he had raced off the porch and thrown himself onto his pony. He was far down the lane before she thought to holler, and too far for him to hear her even if he wanted to.

She felt like sinking right down there on the porch floor and bursting into tears. Instead she made herself go on into the house.

In the kitchen, Claire looked up from the pie dough she was rolling. "Land sakes, child. Sit down. You look like something the cat dragged in."

Hope forced a smile. "That about describes it."

"How's that boy you been with?" Claire asked. "Can he see yet?"

Hope shook her head. "Not yet. The doctors keep saying to be patient."

Claire set a cup of coffee in front of her. "What about his wife?"

SILHOUETTE® DELIVERS FIRST-CLASS ROMANCE— DIRECT TO YOUR DOOR

Mail the Heart sticker on the postpaid order card today and you'll receive:

—4 new Silhouette Romance™ novels—FREE
—a lovely lucite digital clock/calendar—FREE
—and a surprise mystery bonus—FREE

But that's not all. You'll also get:

Free Home Delivery

When you subscribe to Silhouette Romance™, the excitement, romance and faraway adventures of these novels can be yours for previewing in the convenience of your own home. Every month we'll deliver 6 new books right to your door. If you decide to keep them, they'll be yours for only $1.95* each and there is *no* extra charge for postage and handling! There is no obligation to buy—you can cancel at any time simply by writing "cancel" on your statement or by returning a shipment of books to us at our cost.

Free Monthly Newsletter

It's the indispensable insider's look at our most popular writers and their upcoming novels. Now you can have a behind-the-scenes look at the fascinating world of Silhouette! It's an added bonus you'll look forward to every month!

Special Extras—FREE

Because our home subscribers are our most valued readers, we'll be sending you additional free gifts from time to time in your monthly book shipments as a token of our appreciation.

OPEN YOUR MAILBOX TO A WORLD OF LOVE AND ROMANCE EACH MONTH. JUST COMPLETE, DETACH AND MAIL YOUR FREE-OFFER CARD TODAY!

*Terms and prices subject to change without notice.

FREE! lucite digital clock/calendar

You'll love your digital clock/calendar!
The changeable month-at-a-glance calendar
pops out and can be replaced with your
favorite photograph. It is yours FREE as
our gift of love!

Silhouette 💕 Romance®

FREE OFFER CARD

4 FREE BOOKS

FREE HOME DELIVERY

FREE DIGITAL CLOCK/CALENDAR

PLACE
HEART
STICKER
HERE

FREE FACT-FILLED NEWSLETTER

FREE MYSTERY BONUS

MORE SURPRISES THROUGHOUT THE YEAR—FREE

✓ **YES!** Please send me four Silhouette Romance novels, free, along with my free digital clock/calendar and my free mystery gift as explained on the opposite page.

215 CIS HAX5

NAME _____

ADDRESS _____ APT. _____

CITY _____ STATE _____

ZIP CODE _____

MAIL THE POSTPAID CARD TODAY!

PRINTED IN U.S.A.

Remember! To receive your free books, digital clock/calendar and mystery gift, return the postpaid card below. But don't delay!

DETACH AND MAIL CARD TODAY.

If offer card has been removed, write to:
Silhouette Books, 901 Fuhrmann Blvd., P.O. Box 1867, Buffalo, NY 14269-1867

Hope sighed. "He told her he's in traction, and that's why he can't be moved." She sipped at the comforting liquid. "I don't know, Claire."

"Don't know what, honey?" Claire poured herself a cup and sat down across the table.

"It bothers me—this thing I've been doing. Letting Pete think I'm a man. He almost caught me the other day."

"How?"

"Well, when he couldn't stay around to look out for Charlie, I said I'd do it. Then he told me to meet him at the hospital. And when we were both with him, Charlie started to call me Hoble."

Claire's gray eyebrows went up. "What'd you do?"

"I cut him off." Hope sighed again. "I don't like it."

Claire reached across the table. "I know, honey. You're not that kind of person. But it won't be for much longer now. The season's half over."

"If only I could tell Pete the truth."

"You want to tell anyone the truth, it ought to be that boy of yours. He's getting to be a real handful."

"I know. He was waiting for me on the porch. He gave me a real chewing out." Hope rubbed wearily at her forehead. "But you know I can't tell him. It'd get back to Pete for sure." She sighed. "I don't know what's gotten into the boy. Lately he's been so—different."

Claire got to her feet. "He's growing up," she said briskly. "He's changing." She put her empty cup in the sink and went back to her dough. "You think this Charlie's doing right by his wife? Not telling her about his eyes?"

Hope thought with longing of her bed upstairs, of sinking into a sleep that held no problems. "I don't know," she said. "I just don't know. I used to believe that people should always tell the truth. But now . . . I just don't know."

"Now, honey, sometimes you're just too honest for your own good."

Claire's expression was so amusing that Hope had to chuckle. But the situation wasn't funny at all.

"Well," she said, "I don't see how you can call me honest now. I'm lying to Pete. And to Matt. Even to Charlie. And he's lying to his wife. All for the best of reasons." She shook her head. "It just doesn't seem right."

"I think you'd better get up to bed," Claire said. "You been under a lot of tension lately. What you need is a good night's sleep. Things'll look better in the morning."

Hope nodded. She would have liked to think so, but she couldn't see how they could. The lies would still be there. The questions would still be unanswered.

"I ought to wait up for Matt," she said. "We need to talk."

Claire shook her head. "Give the boy time to calm down. You can talk tomorrow."

Hope was too tired to argue. Besides, her mother-in-law was probably right.

The song of a meadowlark woke Hope early the next morning. The sun, shining in through the open window, dappled the old star-of-Bethlehem quilt. Flecks of dust floated in a sunbeam.

She stretched and smiled. Things *did* look better. Maybe she and Matt could take a ride this morning. Maybe they could get back on their old comfortable footing.

Early as it was, Matt was at the table. He glanced up from his bowl of cereal and mumbled a good-morning.

Hope decided to ignore yesterday's outburst. "Isn't it a beautiful day?"

"Yeah." Matt went on eating.

Hope took a sip of coffee. "Want to take a ride together this morning?"

Something happened in Matt's face. At first she thought she saw eagerness, but then his expression hardened.

"I'm riding fence with Hank," he said. "Sorry."

He didn't sound sorry at all, but she clamped her mouth shut. She wasn't about to remind him that he could ride fence any day. If he didn't want to ride with her, that was his right. "Okay," she said. "Maybe another time."

"Yeah. Maybe." Matt had finished his cereal. He took his hat from its peg by the door. He was obviously anxious to be gone. "See you later."

Hope swallowed a sigh as the door closed behind him. Matt was growing so far away from her. Would they ever be able to talk to each other again?

The sharp shrilling of the phone brought her to her feet. "I'll get it in the den," she said, and hurried off, ignoring Claire's knowing smile.

"Hello. Circle C."

"Hello, Hope. You get home okay?"

"Yes, no trouble." It was good to hear his voice. Something inside her responded to the sound of it, felt warmed and comforted, cherished. She liked the feeling a lot.

"Good. Sleep well last night?"

"Pretty well." She wasn't going to tell him she'd missed having his bedtime call to ask about Charlie. Strange how a couple of phone calls could mean so much. "I just wish we'd get some good word on Charlie's eyes."

"Me, too." There was a moment's silence. "Uh, I know you've been away, and you must have a million things to do, but . . ."

There it was again. Why did he hesitate like that? "But what?"

"But I was hoping you might have some free time. Maybe we could take a ride. I haven't had much chance to listen to the stillness lately."

Her heart danced around in her throat, making it hard to talk. "Where are you?"

"Actually, I'm in Havre."

She could almost see that sheepish expression on his face.

"Business, you know."

For a moment she thought of asking him what kind of business brought him so often to such a small town. Was he really there on business, or was he just using that as an excuse to see her? But of course she didn't ask.

"Sure," she said. "Come on out. It's a beautiful day for a ride."

"You're sure it's all right? You're not too busy or anything?"

"I'm sure."

As she hung up the phone, Hope shook her head. It was almost as if he wanted—or expected—to be turned down. Understanding him was a difficult job. She smiled to herself. But it was a job she was willing to take on. Anytime.

An hour later, when he parked his pickup by the porch, she was waiting, two horses already saddled.

The memory of his last kiss, there in the hospital waiting room, reddened her cheeks and turned her insides soft and mushy. She found herself wishing for the feel of his arms again, for the touch of his mouth on hers.

He put out his hand. "Morning, Hope. Good to see you."

"Good morning, Pete." She took the hand he offered and shook it firmly. "I've saddled Blackie for you." She nodded toward the big gelding. "He hasn't been getting much exercise lately."

Pete's eyes went over her shoulder to the pinto mare behind her. "Nice-looking horse."

Hope smiled. "Dixie's a doll. As comfortable as a rocking chair."

She realized suddenly that their hands were still clasped. Awkwardly she withdrew hers. "I guess we'd better get started."

"Just a minute." Pete went to the truck and returned with loaded saddlebags. "I thought we might get hungry. If you can afford to stay out that long, that is?"

"Sure," Hope said. "Sounds good."

For another moment they stood there, simply looking at each other. Then, not knowing what else to do, she turned and swung up onto the mare.

As they rode along, Hope tried to focus on the prairie. Every month it offered particular beauties, and July was no exception. But her thoughts kept coming back to the man beside her.

He looked so good on horseback. As if he'd been born to it. He sat the gelding relaxed and easy, but always in control.

Now and then Hope let herself look at him for more than a second. She liked the blue plaid shirt that matched his eyes, the battered black Stetson that showed real wear, the scuffed boots and the faded jeans. He was an active man. A man to admire. A man to desire. If only...

Longing swept through her with such force that she automatically pulled back on the reins, making Dixie skitter and turn her head to look at her reproachfully.

"Easy girl," she murmured, calming the horse. Calming the horse was easier than calming herself. She had no business thinking such thoughts about him. After all, a couple of kisses didn't mean much to a rodeo cowboy.

In all fairness, she had to admit that Pete wasn't just any cowboy. But even so, what exactly did a couple kisses mean? Maybe she was the only one feeling this longing. Maybe for him it was different.

She yearned to reach out and touch him, if only for a moment. But she didn't dare. And so they rode for some minutes in silence.

"Do you think—" They began the sentence together, and then they both laughed.

"You first," Hope said.

"I was just wondering about Charlie," Pete said. "I don't like to think of the kid in Red Lodge all alone."

Hope nodded. "He isn't. I made sure of that before I left. I called his buddy Rich. The one he usually travels with. He's going down for a few days."

Pete frowned. "I still think we should have told his wife."

Her hands went damp on the reins. There they were, back to the same old subject. She forced her voice to remain calm. "Maybe, but it really wasn't our decision."

"I suppose not." Pete looked grim. "Damn it! Why does life have to be so complicated?"

To her surprise, Hope found herself laughing. "Sorry," she said when he looked at her. "It's just that you sounded so much like Matt when things don't go right for him."

There was that sheepish grin again.

"I suppose I do. But sometimes, well, things just seem more than a man can handle."

Hope stared at him. For some reason she'd thought she was the only one who felt overwhelmed by life.

"What's the matter?" he asked. "Did I put my shirt on backwards?"

She pulled herself together. "No, no." She smiled. "It's just— You always seem like you have everything under control."

The bitterness of his laughter twisted her insides. How much pain had it taken to make him that bitter? How much pain was he still carrying in his heart?

"That's just a front," he said. "Really—" He shrugged.

He didn't go on, and she didn't press him. Some things were too private, too painful.

"Look." He raised a hand to point to a clump of cottonwoods ahead. "Let's stop up there a while."

"Sure." She felt so good being with him. It didn't really matter what they did as long as they were together.

The cottonwood bottom was greener than the surrounding prairie. A little stream had surfaced and, hugging it close, grew cottonwoods and peachleaf willows, tall grasses and huckberry bushes.

Hope swung down from the saddle and ground-tied the mare.

"Over here," Pete said, choosing a grassy spot under a willow.

She sank down where he pointed. What was there about the man that made her feel like a girl on her first date? She scolded herself. She shouldn't even be thinking of this ride as a date. They were friends, and that was all.

But that wasn't all, and she couldn't help knowing it. There was something else between them, something strong, almost magical. She felt its pull as he dropped onto the grass beside her, the saddlebag over one arm.

"Nice place here," he said, setting the food to one side.

She didn't know what to say, how to behave. The air between them seemed charged, the way it was just before a thunderstorm. "Yes," she said, finally. "It's very nice."

Pete looked at her. He hadn't meant to see her again, certainly hadn't meant to come out here and expose himself to temptation. But somehow, someway, he'd ended up in Havre. Talking to her. Inviting himself to her place to ride.

Those big brown eyes of hers were staring at him. She was probably wondering why he was acting such a fool. He should have grabbed her the minute he'd seen her, kissed her good, the way he wanted to—the way she was expecting him to. Her eyes told him she expected that, told him she wanted—

It didn't matter what her eyes told him. He'd promised himself. No involvement. Just friends.

But being just friends with Hope was getting to be nearly impossible. Every time he was close to her it got worse. He wanted to hold her, to protect her. To keep her safe forever. He wanted—to be her man.

Sheer insanity, that was what it was. He was definitely going crazy. Hadn't he promised himself? He was never going to lay himself open to pain like that again.

And here he was.

She was still looking at him, her eyes so inviting. He tried to think of something to say, something to keep him from wanting her. But the only words that came to his mind were words of desire.

She turned away suddenly, her face flushed. Was she feeling it, too? Did she want him?

And then she turned back and his question was answered. Her lips were moist, slightly parted, waiting for his kiss. Under her blue flannel shirt the soft mounds of her breasts rose and fell with her breath.

Slowly, her eyes still on his, she slid down, flat in the prairie grass. For a wild moment he considered throwing himself on top of her, giving vent to the passion that was eating at him. And then, slowly and carefully, he lowered himself beside her.

A good six inches separated their bodies. But lying there, staring at the patches of sky that wavered through the broad leaves of the cottonwood, it was almost as if he could feel her, pulling at him, calling him. She was everything he'd ever wanted. Everything he'd ever dreamed of.

Damnation! She was only a woman. Why did he have to go all softheaded over Hope Crenshaw?

He had no answers, of course. As he stared up at the quivering leaves it was her face he was seeing, her parted lips. Her body, soft, warm, waiting for his. Her eyes, wide and worried, asking questions he had no answers for.

He cursed himself for six kinds of fool. This whole thing was craziness. He should just sit up and take out the food, make some kind of conversation and get his mind on other things.

With a muffled curse he rolled toward her, his body covering hers, his mouth seeking hers. He couldn't help it. He couldn't fight it anymore.

Hope's body strained up toward his, welcoming the feel, the weight of it. She had yearned so long for this. It was good to be finally close to him. She put her arms around his neck, wanting to pull him closer still, needing to feel as much of him as she could.

Her lips welcomed him, too, parting eagerly for the caress of his tongue. It had been so long since that brief kiss in the waiting room.

His touch was tender, then demanding. He rained little kisses over her face, then teased the corner of her mouth.

Her body burned with need of him. She felt his chest, felt the heaviness of his hard thighs, felt his maleness pressing against her.

He put his hands under her back, gathering her up against him as his lips traced the contours of her face, the shape of her ears, the line of her throat.

He shifted himself to lie beside her, and she cried out at the loss, a little whimper against his lips.

"Ssh, shhh, my Hope." His voice was heavy, throaty. It made her feel warm and lazy. Yet inside her pounded this terrible need.

He searched for the buttons of her shirt and laid it open. She shivered in delight as his caresses found trembling flesh.

"So beautiful," he murmured, freeing her breasts and burying his face between them. She felt his mustache and then his lips against her.

Hope felt herself strangely divided. One part of her floated in a sea of sweet desire. That part was willing—eager—to give Pete anything he wanted.

But another part was standing off, looking at what was going on. And that part wasn't floating. That part wasn't happy at all. And in no uncertain terms it told her why.

To give herself to this man, who would probably just walk away afterward, was stupidity. And to do so in the middle of the Circle C range, where someone might come upon them at any moment was crazy as well. Clint would have wanted her to go on with her life, yet Hope wanted more than a moment with Pete Hamilton.

But still she didn't pull back. She'd waited so long. Her need was so strong.

Somehow he'd discarded his shirt. When his body covered hers again, she gasped with pleasure at the feel of his hairy chest against her bare skin.

He fumbled with her belt buckle, reached inside her jeans to stroke the flatness of her stomach and started downward.

"No." At first it was only a whisper, but she forced herself to say it again. "No, Pete, I can't."

He raised his head, raw hunger in his eyes. Hunger and need. His pain twisted through her. She knew that kind of pain so well.

Her need answered his and grew greater. She wanted to forget everything but the two of them, to pull him against her again. But she had to be strong. "Please," she begged. "Please understand. I can't. Not here. Not like this."

His face twisted and changed, emotions chasing each other across it. Finally his features settled into a scowl. "Of course you can't," he said. His voice grated on her raw nerves. "I apologize." He rolled off her and reached for his shirt. With his back turned toward her, he shrugged into it.

"I—" Her lower lip was trembling. She steadied it with her teeth. "I'm sorry." She fumbled with her buttons. God, how would she ever get this stupid shirt closed?

"Nothing for you to be sorry for," he said gruffly. "The fault's all mine."

She couldn't let him think that. It wasn't true. "But Pete, I—"

"I'd rather not talk about it."

His back was still to her. She hesitated, unable to bring herself to agree with him yet sensing that he expected an answer.

"Okay?" he asked.

"Okay," she said finally. He seemed so determined. And she didn't know what else to say.

"Good," he said. "We'll eat."

She finished with the buttons on her shirt and struggled to tuck it into her jeans. How could he expect her to eat after this? How could she even look at him after what had happened?

It was bad enough that she'd let him go so far. But even worse was the knowledge that he could have gone farther. That, in fact, she *wanted* him to go farther. Her whole body flushed with embarrassment at the thought—and ached because she hadn't let him.

A woodpecker drilled high in a nearby cottonwood. Pete tilted his head to look, and she risked a glance at his face. He looked so stern, so angry.

Misery washed over her. She had handled this all wrong. And yet what else could she have done? She was a woman with responsibilities, not a thrill-crazy kid looking for an afternoon of fun.

She took the smallest piece of chicken he offered her, avoiding his eyes. Her mouth was so dry that it was like chewing sawdust. She had to swallow and swallow just to get it down.

The whole lunch was like that. Then they rode in silence back to the ranch. Hope's face felt stiff. She couldn't think of anything to say. She wanted only to cry. But not in front of him. Never in front of him.

Finally they reached the Circle C. When they dismounted, she forced herself to face him. "Thank you for the lunch," she said. "It was very thoughtful of you to bring it."

"Yeah."

His quick scowl and sarcastic tone made the words dry up in her throat. She felt an insane, desperate need to touch him, to explain his pain away. It wasn't that she hadn't wanted to out there. It was only— "Pete, I'm really sorry...." Almost without thinking she reached out, and her fingers grazed his arm.

He jerked back as though she'd burned him. "Forget it," he said. "I'd sure like to."

His words hurt, more than she could have imagined. She cradled her rejected hand, unsure of what to do, knowing only that she cared about this man. And that she wanted, somehow, to make him know it.

Her eyes searched his face, looking for something, she wasn't sure what—some hint that he cared, maybe. But his expression was still grim, still determined.

For a long moment their eyes held. She couldn't let him leave like this. She took one hesitant, faltering step toward him. His face was softening just a little when suddenly Matt came thundering around the corner of the stable on his pony.

He slid to a stop, his gaze turning suspiciously to the stranger. "Hi, Mom. Who's this?"

Hope fought to get control of herself. She couldn't let Matt guess any of what had been happening here. That would only drive him farther away from her.

"This is Mr. Hamilton," she said. "He worked with your father."

Matt leaped to the ground, his face glowing. "You did? Gee. I'm glad to meet you."

As Hope watched, the hard, uncompromising man she'd been facing turned into a warm, compassionate one. "I'm glad to meet you, too, Matt," he said. "Your dad was a great guy. Why, one time we..."

Chapter Eight

On Friday morning, when she piled her gear into the wagon and set off for a two-day rodeo in Butte, Hope thought of old Matt's favorite saying. It seemed very appropriate. She was indeed as edgy as a long-tailed cat in a room full of rocking chairs.

She'd spent the three days since the ride with Pete taking care of ranch business. She'd discussed the purchase of the new bull with Hank and chatted with Claire. And, to her surprise, she'd found her ten-year-old son always underfoot. And filled to bursting with the rodeo stories Pete had told him.

Since Pete had driven away that Monday afternoon with only a brief "Goodbye, Mrs. Crenshaw," Matt's continual comments had been like a sore finger that was always getting banged.

But one good thing had come of it. For a day or two Matt had seemed more like himself. He'd whistled and sang, had even asked her to go for a ride with him.

He'd enjoyed it, too, until he'd found out she was leaving again. And then he went back to being sulky and evading her.

Hope sighed. The long drive to Butte hadn't been much help, full as her mind was of Pete and his strange behavior. "I spend too much time thinking about that man," she told herself as she drove into town. "I ought to just forget him. The way he forgets me."

It had been a while since she'd been to this part of the state. Absently she took note of her surroundings. Butte was a mining town, all right. In spite of the fact that Davis Copper no longer owned it, that mining was no longer done there, the huge headframes that supported the machinery to bring men and materials up out of mines a mile deep were still standing. It was too costly to take them down, she supposed.

Imagine having a mile of earth above your head. She shuddered. She had a rancher's aversion to the thought of working underground, out of the sunlight. She preferred a cow-town like Havre, with the grain elevators and railroad that marked a people living off the land.

And there was another difference. Havre was green, a town of trees and flowers. Butte was a city of dusty reds. Mining pollution had stained its buildings and turned its vegetation stunted and scrawny.

She glanced at her watch. She'd better get over to the motel and check in. This time she'd chosen a place farther from the rodeo grounds. Being found in the same town with Pete too often might make him suspicious. He might even think she was chasing him.

Her face burned. If she knew how to do it, she might *try* chasing him. But as a girl she'd been woefully shy with boys. And after she'd met Clint she hadn't been with other men much.

If only she could figure out what made Pete act the way he did. One minute he treated her as if she were the love of his life, and the next minute as if she were poison.

Wrestling her suitcase out of the back of the car, Hope frowned. First Matt, and now Pete. Sometimes males were impossible.

The rodeo crowd was having fun. The audience loved the excitement of bucking horses, the heart-stopping dangers the contestants faced. They yelled and clapped and cheered, devoured popcorn and peanuts and cotton candy. And held their breath when men hit the sawdust with deadly force.

Hope hitched up her baggy pants and leaned her elbows on the railing. It hardly seemed fair that rodeo performers should risk their lives just so people could have a good time.

But she couldn't blame the crowd. No one was forcing the riders to participate. They did it for fun. Or money. Or to prove themselves men.

Hope frowned. That was another thing she found hard to understand about men. Clint had tried to explain it to her—the sense of triumph he felt in besting the bulls. For him it was a great thrill, a really worthwhile accomplishment.

But try as she might she had never been able to see it that way, to feel what he was feeling. For her it was just a job, and a dirty and dangerous one at that.

Take the young cowboy who had just been carted away to the hospital with a broken arm. He was lucky it was just his arm. Rodeo riders rarely made it through a season without injury. Broken bones were everyday things to them. And this cowboy, a brash nineteen-year-old who reminded her of Charlie Rivers, would be back on a bucking horse long before his arm—it was his left, and he was right-handed—was fully healed.

There was no lack of men ready to face the dangers of the arena. She supposed there never would be. In a country like this, with its frontier tradition, there would always be someone willing, even eager, to court danger.

Under the curly yellow wig, a prickle raised the hair on the back of her neck. Gooseflesh rippled the skin on her arms. Hope shivered. Pete Hamilton was someplace nearby. And he was getting closer. He was the kind of danger that made her life exciting.

He came up behind her. "Evening, Hobie." He leaned against the railing beside her, his shoulder inches from hers.

His voice made her body go warm with memories of those moments on the prairie. Thank goodness the bright face paint hid her flushing features. "Evening, boss," she said, trying to keep her voice relaxed.

He waited, but she didn't turn to look at him. He cursed himself for being so stupid. Why didn't he just stay away from her? Why did he torture himself like this?

"Some real good rides this afternoon," he said, feeling like an idiot. He wanted to tell her what was really on his mind, wanted to apologize for that fiasco under the cottonwoods. He wasn't some fly-by-night horse jockey carving notches on his pistol. He wanted to be sure she knew that.

He felt his body growing warmer. Lord, but it had been good there, with the prairie stillness around them and her in his arms. Holding her, feeling her against him. He'd almost forgotten what being with a woman was like. It had been such a long time.

Risking a glance at her, he wished he knew how much money she needed to get that ranch back on a steady footing. If only there were some way he could get it to her. He wanted her out of the arena, away from Old Devil Eyes and his kind.

"Rodeo's a funny business," she said. "Why do they do it? Risk injury and everything like they do?"

"Money," he suggested, since he was thinking about it.

She shook her head. "Not enough money for everyone."

She was right. "To be a champion, then," he said.

"Everybody doesn't make it to a silver buckle."

He knew that. Every rodeo cowboy did. "No, but a man's got to try. He's got to know he gave it his best."

Standing there, shoulder-to-shoulder with her, he felt the heat of her body. He remembered the silky smoothness of her flesh, the blueness of the veins beneath her creamy skin. The rosy pink—

"And if his best isn't good enough?" she asked.

Pete shrugged, wishing he could close the distance between them. It was maddening being so close and not being able to touch her. He swallowed a sigh. "At least he knows he tried."

She was silent again. He wondered what she was thinking. Was she wondering about the bulls coming up? Was she worrying that he would find her out? Was she enjoying being close to him?

He knew one thing. In spite of the torture of it, he didn't want to leave her side. Just standing near her gave him a good feeling, sort of like coming home after a long time on the road.

"What's the word on Charlie?" she asked.

He sighed, some of his good feeling going. He was really worried about that one. "The same. Nothing new. The kid's having a rough time of it."

"Yeah."

The bitterness in her voice cut at him. For a second he was yanked back to that terrible time after Annie's accident. His stomach tightened and his mouth went dry as panic hit him.

But he pulled himself out of it. He'd survived it then and he would survive it now. "Life's like that," he said quietly. "We have to take our chances. Nothing's for sure."

She shrugged. "Yeah, I know. Like they say, nothing's certain but death and taxes."

It came to him then, one way he could help her. It was so easy, he didn't know why he hadn't thought of it before. "Speaking of taxes," he said, carefully keeping his eyes on the arena, "you're going to be paying more. Soon."

He heard the sharp intake of her breath. Damn! How could he be so clumsy at this? He hadn't meant to scare her.

"What do you mean?" she asked.

"You're doing such a good job," he hurried to explain, "I decided you ought to have a raise. Starting this week."

There was a long moment of silence. Finally she spoke. "Gee, boss, that's great. But are you sure—"

"I'm sure," he said, making his voice firm. The rodeo committee would never know he was making up the difference himself. He would double her wages, triple them if he could. Anything to get her out of the arena sooner, away from those damned bulls.

He could understand Clint teaching her to clown. He'd probably figured that would help her over her fear for him. But how had the man stood it, watching her face the meanest bulls around?

And then he saw what he'd been missing. Clint had been in there with her. He hadn't had to stand helplessly by, watching with his heart in his mouth, knowing that if something went wrong he would never be able to get down there in time.

For a moment he let himself imagine coming home to the Circle C at night. Hope waiting for him on the weather-beaten porch, a smile of welcome on her face, a kiss waiting on her lips. And the boy galloping up on his pony, his face glowing, yelling, "Hi, Pete. Glad you're home."

But the picture dissolved in a flash of gut-wrenching pain, and he saw Annie's tearstained face when she'd told him that she needed room to breathe and that she was leaving.

He swallowed hard. Even Annie hadn't known how final that goodbye would be.

If only he'd stopped her, he told himself for the hundred-thousandth time. But he knew, deep in his heart, that he couldn't have stopped her for long. Not

Annie. She had always been hell-bent on having her own way. Right or wrong had made no difference to her.

Hope stood beside him, scarcely daring to breathe. Her thoughts chased each other in endless futile circles. She wanted to know how big the raise was. She wanted to know why he'd given it to her. She wanted to know a hundred different things.

But she was afraid to ask, afraid to try to talk to him. How could she pretend to be Hobie when she was feeling this way?

Desire thickened her tongue. It heated her body. She gripped the railing in front of her. If he didn't move away soon she didn't know what she would do. The compulsion to touch him was almost overwhelming. She wanted to turn into his arms, to feel his warm closeness against her. The memory of his kisses, of his gentle, loving hands, was almost more than she could bear.

She started counting backward in her mind. If she didn't do something to distract herself she was going to have to touch him. She shifted the weight of her body. Maybe she could edge closer, brush against him.

"Well," he said, "I just thought I'd let you know." Then he was gone, leaving her so weak in the knees that it was a darn good thing she didn't have to face any bulls for a long time.

* * *

Back in the motel room after the show was over, she paced the narrow floor. Thank goodness one season on the circuit would let her replace Sultan. She didn't know how long she could take this kind of life.

She threw herself down on the bed. It hadn't been this bad when she and Clint had traveled together. After she'd gotten over her initial fear and learned to face the bulls, they'd had fun. Matt had enjoyed it, too, young as he'd been then. Traveling around in their little trailer had been a big adventure.

But that seemed like hundreds of years ago. Ranch life was better. She flopped over on the bed and pounded the rumpled pillow. After this season was over she would be glad, real glad, to settle down and lead a normal life again. She sighed. If only Pete would get the same idea.

Of course, he was so used to being on the road he probably liked it. She rolled the other way and pounded the pillow again. Even if he didn't, what made her think he would want to settle down with her?

Well, he wanted her. Or he had out there on the prairie. But that didn't mean much. She wasn't so inexperienced that she would let herself mistake passion for love. Marriage needed more than wanting. Marriage needed love. And commitment. And trust.

It was marriage she wanted. She had no doubts about that.

Double damnation! She threw the pillow on the floor. She felt like stomping on it or ripping it to shreds, but that would hardly be an adult thing to do. Sighing, she bent down and retrieved it.

It always got back to this thing about Hobie. Could Pete sense that she was keeping something from him? Could that be the reason for his stop-and-go attitude toward her? Maybe she should tell him the truth. She'd thought about it often enough. But how could she tell him now, after all this time?

As usual, there were no answers to any of her questions.

She twisted and turned in the unfamiliar bed. How could she know what was right to do? How was a person supposed to decide things like this?

Take Charlie Rivers, for example. He wasn't telling Mary Lou the truth about his eyes. Was he right in trying to protect her? Or would it just make matters worse? How on earth could he tell?

And what about Matt? Was she wrong not to let him know what she was doing? But there was no way they could keep her identity secret if Matt found out she was fighting bulls. He would have to tell his best friend, Jimmy. Or he would let something slip to Hank. There was just no way she could let him in on it and expect the secret to stay a secret.

She flopped over again. With a muffled exclamation she sat up and began untangling the sheet that was twisted around her ankles. Why am I doing this? she asked herself in irritation. Why don't I just go to sleep?

This time she knew the dream for what it was. The bull's eyes were red neon, and his coat glowed with an evil reddish cast. And fury marked every line of his outraged body.

Up in the stands, the huge rodeo crowd held its collective breath, waiting to see what the clown would do.

Reaching for the familiar red suspenders, Hope suffered a shock. She was out in the arena, all right, but she wasn't wearing her clown outfit. No baggy pants. No polka-dot shirt. Nothing but a pair of flimsy pink baby-doll pajamas.

The bull pawed the ground. His eyes shifted as he considered his next move. Not *whether* he was going to kill her. *How.*

She tried to think. What would Clint do? But her mind was stuck. Over and over it kept repeating, "I'm wearing my pajamas. I'm wearing my pajamas."

Some part of her knew she was dreaming, recognized that this couldn't be real. But another part was terrified.

The bull's eyes held her. Like the eyes of some apparition out of hell, they paralyzed her will, kept her motionless. She was at his mercy.

And then, out of the corner of her eye, she saw movement. Pete was coming toward her! She tried to cry out, to warn him away, out of danger, but no words would come.

He came right up to her, his face shining with welcome. He came and stood in front of her as though the bull didn't even exist.

She couldn't see the bull anymore. Pete's body blocked it from view. But she heard him, heard the snort that signaled he was ready to charge.

She felt Pete's hands on her shoulders, drawing her close. But she pushed against him, pushed with all her might. As he fell aside, out of the way, she saw the bull coming at her. It was too late to save herself. The huge curved horns dipped and reached out for her. Hooked—

Her scream brought her violently awake. She clutched the covers in a cold sweat and willed herself to stop shaking. The dream had been so vivid, so terrifying. She'd dreamed of the bulls before, before Clint had become a clown. Before he'd taken her into the arena with him to teach her not to be afraid.

But in those dreams the bull had always been after Clint. When she'd started facing them herself, the dreams had stopped.

She shivered. There was no denying that Pete meant an awful lot to her. But why should she imagine him standing between her and the bull? That didn't make much sense.

With a sigh she rearranged the covers yet again. The bed was beginning to look like a trampled arena, and she was getting no sleep at all.

She wanted this summer to be over. Being in the arena didn't scare her as it once had. Even with these dreams. But it was not a life she could really enjoy.

Learning Clint's techniques had been easy, but she hadn't absorbed his attitude, his philosophy toward what he did so well.

Certainly she had no trouble believing that she was smarter than the bulls. Except for an occasional second when she was staring into one's eyes.

But she couldn't see why that was so all-fired important. Or why she should have to go on proving it indefinitely, as the men said they did. She just wanted to be through with this kind of life.

Chapter Nine

When she got up the next morning, Hope called the hospital in Red Lodge. She'd been calling as Hobie every morning to get the news on Charlie.

This morning the young cowboy sounded really down. "They took the bandages off," he told her. "And the doc says I ought to be seeing soon. But Hobie, I'm scared. I heard them talking to each other yesterday. The longer this goes on, the less chance I have of my sight coming back."

"Quit thinking like that," Hope said briskly. "It's not allowed."

Charlie's laugh was brittle, but it was a laugh. "Yes, sir. It's only that, I just wish—"

"Wish what?"

"Aw, you're in Butte. I ought to be there, too. I was counting on being with Mary Lou. She says she's all right, but ..."

"But what?"

"What if she's doing what I'm doing?" Charlie's voice started to go up in panic. "What if something's wrong and she's not telling me? Trying to protect me?"

Hope sighed again. It seemed very possible. "I don't know."

"Listen, Hoble, I wouldn't ask you, but you're right there. I mean, could you just stop around and see her? Tell me how she looks? It'd mean an awful lot to me. It'd put my mind at rest."

Hope hesitated. It would take some tall explaining—her showing up instead of the man Mary Lou would obviously expect. She couldn't very well go over to the house in clown costume.

But she couldn't deny Charlie this, not when she knew it would make him feel better. "Okay," she said. "I'll try to see her this morning. Give me the address."

The little house was surrounded by beds of blooming flowers. It had a friendly look, almost as though it reflected the love within it. The young woman who opened the door moved slowly and clumsily, but her face, under her mop of shining red curls, was radiant.

"I'm so glad you called. It's been driving me crazy not being able to get to Charlie."

She motioned Hope into the small living room and lowered her bulk into a chair. "The doctor says we're going to make it this time." She rested a hand on her smock. "Sure has been a long wait."

Her eyes went to Hope's face. "Is my Charlie really all right?"

Hope swallowed. She had to be careful. "Yes. Sure. Why do you ask?"

Mary Lou frowned. "I don't know. Something about his voice."

Hope managed a little smile. "He misses you. And he wants to be here. For the baby's arrival."

Mary Lou sighed. "Lord knows I want that, too. He's supposed to coach me during labor. But it doesn't seem likely. He doesn't even know how much longer he'll be in traction."

Hope's mind raced. Wouldn't Mary Lou be better off knowing the truth? Shouldn't Charlie be there for his child's birth?

She swallowed a sigh. It was up to Charlie to decide. Just as she had to decide about Pete and about Matt.

"He's worried about you," Hope said. "That's why he asked me to come. To give him a firsthand report."

Mary Lou frowned again. "He said he was going to ask Hobie Brown to come. You know, that clown that kept the bull away from him. How come you came instead?"

Hope swallowed again. None of her carefully contrived explanations seemed suitable. How was she going to get around this?

And suddenly there seemed only one way. "Mary Lou," she said, "it's like this. I'm Hobie the clown."

Mary Lou's eyes widened. "Charlie didn't tell me that—"

"That I'm a woman. That's because he doesn't know. He's only seen me in costume."

"But why?"

"I needed work. They said I looked too fragile."

Mary Lou grinned. "So you decided to show them."

"Something like that—" Hope began.

The chime of the doorbell interrupted her. "More company." Mary Lou grinned and heaved herself to her feet. "I'll be right back."

As she waited, Hope wondered if she'd done the right thing. Mary Lou was so young. Could she keep the secret?

Hope sighed. She was so tired of secrecy, of having to think before she opened her mouth. She'd never lived like this before. She wanted to go back to the truth, to—

"Why, Mr. Hamilton! What a surprise!"

Hope's heart turned a somersault. Pete! What was he doing here?

"Come on in," Mary Lou was saying. "This must be my day for company." She paused in the doorway. "You know Mrs. Crenshaw, don't you?"

This time Hope's heart threatened to stay upside down. If Mary Lou let slip what she knew...

"Yes. Hello, Hope." His voice was even, noncommittal. She could be any chance acquaintance.

"Hello, Pete." She hoped her voice was steadier than her knees. "How are you?"

"Doing fairly well," he said.

Her eyes searched his face, but there was no clue to his feelings about her. He just looked his normal, friendly self.

"Sit down," Mary Lou said, lowering herself once more into her chair. "Mrs. Crenshaw just came around to check up on me for Charlie."

Hope nodded. "I called to see how he was doing. And when he heard I was in Butte—"

"What *are* you doing here?" Pete asked.

Hope saw Mary Lou's startled glance. Oh, please, she begged, don't let her blurt it out. "Oh, more ranch business. I'm looking for a new bull." She managed a little laugh. "Hopefully this one will have enough smarts not to get caught in a dry wash in a downpour."

Pete nodded. If he thought it strange that she was looking for a bull in a mining town, he didn't say so. He turned instead to Mary Lou. "Charlie knew the rodeo was here this weekend," he said. "He asked me to come see how you are, too."

Mary Lou grinned. "That boy just won't believe that I'm fine and dandy." Her grin faded, and she brought her hands to her rounded abdomen. "Sure wish he could come home, though. Doc says this one could arrive early."

Pete smiled. "Then you'll like my news. Charlie should be home in a week or so."

Mary Lou's eyes filled with tears. "For real?"

"Yes," Pete said. "For real."

Hope bit her lower lip. Could Charlie have regained his eyesight since she'd talked to him? But something about Pete told her that wasn't so. Pete looked almost grim, as though he meant to insist that Charlie come home. No matter what.

They chatted for a while longer, telling Mary Lou all they could while skirting the truth. Then Pete rose. "I've got to be going," he said. "You can be sure I'll give Charlie a good report."

Mary Lou struggled to her feet. "Thank you. And thank you for coming. It helps a lot."

Hope rose, too. "It's time for me to leave, too," she said.

Mary Lou smiled. "Could you wait for just a minute?" She turned to Pete. "Just a little girl talk," she said. "You understand?"

Pete nodded and started toward the door. Then he stopped and turned toward Hope. "Ah, if you're not busy tonight . . . maybe we could have a late dinner. After the show."

She had to swallow twice before she could answer him. "Yes, I'd like that. I'm at the Best Western, on North Wyoming."

Pete nodded. "I'll call you later, then." He shook Mary Lou's hand and was gone.

Watching him stride out to his pickup, Hope smiled to herself. So it wasn't over. She was going to have dinner with Pete. Another lovely dinner. Another chance—

"I see!" Mary Lou's exclamation startled her, and she turned to see the young woman grinning at her. "Pete doesn't know you're Hobie," Mary Lou said.

"No," Hope replied. "He doesn't. I really needed the job because of that bull."

Mary Lou chuckled. "And you're Pete's new woman. The one Charlie's been hearing about." She clapped her hands together. "Just wait till my Charlie hears this. He's been buddying with a woman and didn't even know it."

"Please . . ." Hope began.

Mary Lou put an arm around her shoulders and squeezed. "Don't you worry," she said. "Me and Charlie, we know how to keep a secret." She frowned. "But I bet Pete wouldn't like it one little bit. If he finds out, the manure's really going to fly!"

* * *

Sitting across the table from Pete after the show, Hope tried to calm her nerves. This was worse than facing a bull. At least she knew the bull's motives. He wanted to stomp her, gore her, eliminate her. She didn't have to guess. The bull was honest about his feelings.

But with Pete... She didn't know how he felt about her. What he wanted from her. She didn't know what to say or do. Most of all she was afraid of saying the wrong thing and giving away her secret.

And then there was how he made her feel. He looked so good in his raspberry silk shirt and his faded jeans. A lock of curly hair had fallen over his forehead. She longed to push it back. She longed to touch him. But none of that was possible. Not after what had happened out on the prairie.

She shifted nervously on the chair. The new dress that she'd stopped for on her way back to the motel— maybe it was too much. Maybe he would guess she'd bought it especially for him.

Stop it, she told herself, smoothing the full skirt of deep blue silk. She hadn't had a new dress in years. And it had been on sale.

Besides, she'd been given another chance to be with him.

Finally getting a grip on her thoughts, she asked the question that had been on her mind all day. "Why did you tell her Charlie would be home in a week?"

He looked up from the menu, and his mouth tightened. "Because he will."

"But his eyes—"

Pete's face grew grimmer. "That woman needs him. He's supposed to be there when the baby's born. He's her childbirth coach."

"But his eyes. And his leg."

"Hell and damnation!" People at adjoining tables looked up, and Pete lowered his voice. "He doesn't need his leg to coach her, or his eyes, either." He straightened his shoulders. "He's going to be there. And that's that."

His gaze defied her to contradict him, but she had no intention of trying. "I think you're right," she said. "He shouldn't miss the baby's birth. No matter what."

She noticed his surprise. He *had* expected her to fight him on this. "But how are you going to convince him? He's a pretty stubborn fellow."

Pete's smile was like sunrise over the prairie. If only he were there to smile at her like that every morning.

"First I'll try persuasion," he said. "After all, I'm a reasonable man."

She shook her head. "Maybe you are. I don't think Charlie is. It just won't work."

He shrugged. "Then I'll try threats. No more rodeoing."

Hope shook her head. "There are other circuits, Pete. You can't keep him off them all."

He sighed. "Then I'll just tell him that that's the way it is. He goes home and tells Mary Lou. Or *I* go tell her."

She gave him a hard look. "He sure isn't going to like *that*."

He shrugged, his mouth setting in that firm line. "A man's got to do what he thinks is right. And it's right for that boy to go home. I know it and you know it."

Pete felt warmed by her nod of approval, by the admiration in those big brown eyes. Somehow he'd felt she would be against his plan. To find that she wasn't made him feel like flying. Or maybe it was just being able to look at her pretty face. Her eyes all warm with feeling for Charlie and Mary Lou. Her lips half parted in a smile.

Longing surged through him, longing so strong that he had to grit his teeth to keep from acting on it. He wanted to feel those lips under his own, that body against his.

He turned his attention to the menu. If only she believed in telling *him* the truth. This thing between them was tearing him apart. Or maybe it was seeing her out there with the bulls and not being able to stop her.

It was later that he somehow got to talking about Annie, about his marriage. "She was young. Wild. She wanted the whole world."

Hope watched him, waiting, her eyes wide. He found himself going on. "First off, she wanted a championship cowboy." He shrugged. "She got me without too much trouble." He swallowed. It was painful remembering, but somehow he wanted Hope to know. "Then she wanted more."

"More *what*?"

He liked the inflection in her question, as though she thought having him would be enough for any woman. He forced himself to go on. "More money. More excitement. More fun."

He was silent for a moment, gathering his thoughts, the perceptions he'd pieced together so painfully. "They explained it to me in Al-Anon. After— Her daddy was a heavy drinker. So was her mama. When her mama died, her daddy took Annie on the road with him. He was in trouble a lot. She grew up with it."

Hope shook her head. "I don't think I understand."

"I didn't, either. But they say that kids like that get used to lives full of crisis. To constant excitement. They need it. So they make their own. Annie was good at that. Real, real good."

He sipped his coffee, remembering. "She lied and cheated and drank too much. She said it made her life bearable."

Hope waited, almost holding her breath. She could hardly believe that he was telling her all this, letting her see so much of his private self.

"I tried to stop her," he went on. "I tried everything I knew." His voice fell, and he hesitated. "But nothing worked. Then one night we had a bad fight. She said she was leaving me and raced off in her pickup."

His voice grew choked. "They found it next morning. Wrapped around a tree. She was dead."

"Oh, Pete. I'm so sorry." She reached across the table to take his hand. "How awful for you."

He dropped his head, hiding his face. "I—I just can't stand to see these kids lying to each other." His voice was heavy with pain. "Lying will ruin their marriage. I know. Whatever's wrong, they've got to face it. Together."

Hope's heart pounded. She had to tell him before they got involved in any more lies, before this thing between them went any farther. What a relief it would be to have everything out in the open. To share it all with him.

"I just couldn't stand it," he said, his grip tightening on her hand until she thought her bones would break. "Not if someone I loved lied to me again."

The words hit her like a sudden blow and took her breath away. She knew she couldn't go through with it. If she told him the truth she would lose him. It was that simple. Not only would she lose him, she would lose the ranch and that was Matt's heritage.

She would just have to hang on. There was nothing else to do. Hang on until Labor Day. That was only six or seven weeks. Just hang on.

By Labor Day she should have enough money for the new bull. After that show, Hobie the clown could vanish. Maybe... But there was no telling what Pete would do.

"When are you going to see Charlie?" she asked, wanting to change to a less sensitive subject.

His mouth tightened again. "First thing tomorrow, if I can. I mean to have him home by Monday or Tuesday."

Hope nodded. She just hoped they would keep her secret—Charlie and Mary Lou.

She and Pete spent the rest of the meal talking about other, less personal things. It was late when they returned to the motel.

"I'll walk you in," Pete said, and she didn't argue. She was reluctant to give up his company. It had been a pleasant evening, talking about ranch life, about raising horses and cattle, about the joy of living in the West.

They stopped in front of her door. Her heart was jumping around again, and her body was remembering the day on the prairie. If he kissed her again, if he asked to come in...

She smiled to herself. Everything to do with her clowning was carefully packed away, out of sight. This time would be perfect. This time she was ready to give him—

"Thank you for the dinner," she said, tilting her head to look up into his eyes. They were warm, but in the dimness of the hall she could read nothing else in them.

"Thank you," he said. "I always enjoy your company."

For a moment they stood, lost in each other's gazes. He took one hesitant step backward, away from her. Without thinking she covered the space between them, put her arms around his neck and, lifting herself up on tiptoe, kissed him.

At first his lips were stiff—with surprise, she supposed. But then they warmed and softened and he took over direction of the kiss. His tongue went looking for hers and his arms enfolded her, drawing her up against him, so close she had to fight for breath.

It was a totally satisfying kiss. It left her feeling wonderfully warmed and wanted. A living, loving woman.

He took the key from her fingers and pushed open the door. "Hope—"

"Ssh." She kissed the word off his lips and drew him into the room with her. "It's all right," she whispered. This was their safe place, this room, shut off from the world and all its problems.

He kissed her again, his hands pressing her to him. His lips traced the contours of her face, tickled her earlobe, teased the corner of her mouth.

Desire flamed through her, warming her blood, twisting her insides into a tightly coiled spring. She wanted him. She wanted to be his—in the ultimate union of male and female. Nothing else mattered. Nothing else existed.

Her body melted into his. Her curves blended into his angles.

And then it happened. He lifted his mouth away from hers and let go of her body.

She reached out, her hands on his chest, to steady herself. "Pete?" The word was half whimper, half plea.

She felt the drumming of his heart under her fingers. She heard the harsh unevenness of his breathing.

"Pete, what is it?"

The question hung in the air between them. He wanted her. She knew that, had felt his readiness, his need. But something...

His voice was low, husky. "Hope, I...I've gotta go."

He seemed to struggle with words, then gave up. "See you."

She sank down on the bed, her knees gone limp, as the door closed behind him. How, she asked herself, how had this happened? Again. But again there was no answer.

Chapter Ten

The drive to Drummond took up most of the next morning. Hope moved in a kind of daze, doing what needed to be done and afterward not remembering how or when.

The Sunday crowd enjoyed the brilliant July weather, the excitement of the riding events. But Hope couldn't respond to the electricity in the air or the enjoyment of the people around her. She was tuned in to only one person. And Pete Hamilton didn't make an appearance the entire day.

So, heading home for Havre when the show was over, Hope had plenty to think about. Not only his abrupt departure from her room and his plan to force

Charlie to tell his wife the truth, but the fact that he'd missed the Drummond show.

Hope sighed and wriggled her shoulders to ease the tension. She still wasn't completely sure if Pete had the right to make that choice for Charlie. After all, she'd always believed that a person should have the right to choose for himself. In theory that seemed simple enough.

But look at Annie. Judging by what Pete had told her, Annie's right to choose had cost her her life. Charlie's might in the long run have cost him his marriage—or, if he made a different choice, the life of his unborn child.

Hope felt tears welling up in her eyes. Was that why Pete hadn't been in Drummond? Had he gone to Red Lodge to lay it on the line with Charlie?

She thought of Mary Lou's bright face, of the love that radiated from her. Charlie should be with her, not stuck off by himself in a lonely hospital room. But—

Double double double damnation! Hope pounded the steering wheel in frustration. Sometimes she wished her vocabulary of swear words was bigger. Especially lately, when everything seemed to be closing in on her.

She turned her head, slowly tensing and untensing the muscles in her shoulders. Her neck was stiffening up, and she had a long way to go.

She was no closer to any answers when she pulled into the yard at the ranch. There was no sign of Matt, but lights were burning in the living room.

Claire looked up from her knitting. "Hi, honey. You look beat."

Hope dropped her bag by the door and fell into a chair. "I am. Where's Matt?"

"He's spending the night at Jimmy's. His folks took them into town to see some movie about the Old West."

Tired as she was, Hope smiled at Claire's expression. She knew what was coming next.

"Just can't understand those Hollywood fellows. The West wasn't ever like they make out."

Hope chuckled. "You'll just have to set Matt straight." She leaned back in the chair and tried to relax. Every muscle she owned seemed to be screaming in protest.

"Any phone calls?" she asked, voicing the question that had been in the back of her mind for the last couple of hours.

Claire shook her head. "No, Hamilton didn't call. You hear any more news about that blind boy?"

The question made Hope's stomach lurch. "Mom, he's not blind."

Claire looked stubborn. "A body that can't see is blind. Nothing else to call it."

Hope was too tired to argue. Besides, when Claire made up her mind about something, there was no un-making it.

"I talked to him yesterday," Hope said. "He asked me to go see his wife. Find out how she was doing."

"And?"

"And I did. She's a nice girl, Mom. They deserve to be happy."

"Most people don't seem to deserve the troubles they get," Claire said, her needles flying. "But they get them anyhow."

She eyed her daughter-in-law. "And speaking of troubles, you got enough of your own without bor-rowing other people's."

Hope didn't argue with that, either. "I suppose so." She pulled herself to her feet. "Listen, I'm going up to bed. Talk to you in the morning."

"Right." Claire looked up from her knitting. "You got a week at home this time? Before you head out for Stanford?"

"Yes."

"Better work in some time for Matt."

Hope sighed, wondering what the boy had been doing now. "I will, Mom," she promised. "I will."

Her own bed felt wonderful, but sleep refused to come. Her thoughts whirled in a merry-go-round of confusion. Had Pete been to Red Lodge already? And if he had, what had happened there?

Again she had no answers. She stared up at the ceiling, watching the shadows of the cottonwood leaves outside her window moving in the moonlight. If only she could call Pete. But he'd given her his office number, not his number at home. Besides, she wasn't sure she could bring herself to call him at home even if she had the number.

In the darkened room she lay laughing at herself. Every day she routinely faced raging bulls, but the thought of phoning a man sent her stomach into a tizzy.

Sleep came, finally, but when she woke the next morning she felt as if she'd fought a bull and he'd won. She dragged herself out of bed and took a hot shower.

The water beating down on her had a soothing effect, and when she went down to breakfast she felt more like her normal self.

The phone rang just as she was pouring her second cup of coffee.

Claire smiled. "Better take it in the den."

Hope's hand trembled as she reached for the receiver. It was probably someone else—Matt wanting to be picked up, or—

"Hello, Circle C."

"Hello, Hope."

Her heart bounced up into her throat and then down again. "Hello, Pete."

"I, ah . . . hate to bother you like this. But I need a favor."

"Oh?" Her mind raced. "What kind of favor?"

"Well, I've talked Charlie into going home. But he wants someone to be there with Mary Lou when he gets there. A woman. She told him how much she liked you. And, well, I've hired an ambulance and I'm going to follow them. But Charlie wants to know if you'll meet us there."

Hope tried to think. "It'll take me—"

"There's plenty of time," Pete went on. "The doctors aren't letting him go till tomorrow. They've still got some more tests to run." There was a pause. "I know you're busy, and I wouldn't ask you, but..."

Hope swallowed a sigh. It meant another long drive, more weary hours on the road, another lonely night in a motel. But there was really no way she could refuse. She knew what it was like to be alone, to have lost father and mother. "Yes," she said. "Of course I'll come."

"Good."

She heard the relief in his voice.

"Listen," he said. "I'll make you a reservation. At the Copper King Inn on Harrison. It's near the house. The rodeo will pay the charges."

"But—"

"We have funds for these things. You know that."

She saw there was no use in arguing. "All right. What time do you expect to get into Butte tomorrow?"

"Probably around noon. There's the release papers to be signed and all. I'd go over to the house in midmorning, though."

"What'll I tell Mary Lou?" The more she thought about it the more nervous she felt.

"Charlie's already called her. He, ah . . . he told her I wanted to meet you there. They've got some idea that . . . that is . . ."

She could visualize his sheepish expression. What did he expect her to say? She smiled grimly. He'd gotten himself into this tight spot and he could just get himself out. She had no intention of rushing to the rescue. In fact, some imp made her say, "I don't understand. What idea do they have?"

There was a long silence. It lasted so long that she wondered if he would ever break it. Maybe he would just hang up.

When he finally spoke, his voice was weak. "They think that we . . . that I . . . that we've been seeing each other."

"Oh, well, we have." Let him handle that, she thought.

"Yes, but—" He faltered, then struggled on. "They think we're really serious. That is . . ."

Suddenly she couldn't take any more of this. These on-and-off games of his were driving her crazy. Let him have a taste of his own medicine.

"Well," she said briskly, "we sure don't want them to get the wrong idea. I'll see you there. 'Bye."

She hung up. Let him think about that for a while! And she stomped off upstairs to throw some clothes in a bag and write a note to Matt.

Butte was just as dusty red as ever, and she was just as lonely. But she made it through the long evening and the longer night, and the next morning at ten she arrived at the Rivers's house.

"Come in," Mary Lou said. "I'm real glad to see you."

Hope followed her into the living room.

"Sure am glad Charlie's coming home."

Hope nodded. "I bet you are."

"Oh, and Mrs. Crenshaw..."

"Call me Hope, please."

Mary Lou smiled. "Well, Hope, don't you worry none. We won't spill your secret." She grinned. "Charlie was real flabbergasted when he found out old Hobie was a woman. You should have heard him laugh. But he still says you're the best bullfighting clown he's ever worked with."

Hope managed a smile. This was worse than facing the bulls. Her nerves were all shot. And she wasn't sure if she was more anxious over Charlie's arrival or over seeing Pete again.

Mary Lou was eyeing her critically. "You look kind of peaked," she said. "Something wrong?"

Hope was almost thrown into a panic. "No, no..." she said. "It's just, well . . . Pete and I had a little disagreement the other night."

Mary Lou nodded. "Me and Charlie don't have disagreements. We have fights. Real loud ones." She flashed Hope a smile. "But we always make up. You will, too."

Hope nodded. "You're probably right."

By lunchtime she'd relaxed a little, but Mary Lou was growing tenser. "I can't wait to see him," she said. "It seems so long. You don't think something's happened?"

Hope shook her head. "Of course not. You know how hospitals are. There's always some kind of delay."

"Yeah, I know. It's just– " Mary Lou leaned forward in the chair. "Is that—?"

Hope went to the window. "Yes, it's them."

She followed Mary Lou to the door. Their moment of truth was upon them. She only hoped Mary Lou could handle it.

"Charlie, Charlie, honey!"

Charlie looked up from between the men who were helping him and smiled. "Hello, baby."

His eyes were no longer bandaged and for a moment Hope thought he'd regained his sight. But then she realized he was responding to Mary Lou's voice.

Behind him she glimpsed Pete, wearing a worried frown. She sympathized with him. There could be a lot of trouble.

The ambulance men got Charlie installed on the couch and went on their way. Mary Lou eased herself down beside him. "Oh, Charlie."

Hope turned away. It seemed almost indecent to watch such an emotional reunion.

But she couldn't go too far. Any minute now Charlie would tell his wife the truth. Any minute now she might be needed.

Pete came back in from seeing the ambulance men off. He stood by the front door, waiting, obviously as ill at ease as she was.

"Wish this was over with," he mumbled, half to himself.

Suddenly she found that she was no longer miffed at him for leaving her room as he had. "Me, too," she echoed.

She reached out and touched his arm. They were in this thing together, and they would see it through together, as well.

He took one of her hands in his tentatively. She left it there. At that moment she was desperately in need of the comfort of his touch. So much could go wrong.

From behind them came the mumble of voices. Then a quick gasp and Mary Lou's "Charlie, no!"

Hope moved closer to Pete, drawing on his strength while she waited. But there were no screams, no hysterics. Just the quiet murmur of voices again.

And then Charlie called, "Pete, Hope. Would you come here?"

They went, their hands still entwined.

Mary Lou looked up at them, her eyes bright with tears. "Thank you," she said. "For getting him to come home. I knew something was wrong. I felt it. Something." She wiped at the tears on her cheeks. "It's better to know."

Charlie nodded. "You were right, Pete. Thanks."

Pete and Hope smiled together. Hope felt relief pouring over her, leaving her weak in the knees.

"There's just one thing," Charlie said. "One more favor."

"Of course." Pete beat her by a second in replying.

"Wonder if you could take us to the hospital? Looks like our little one is on the way."

"You mean—" Hope began.

Mary Lou heaved herself to her feet. "I was already having pains before they got here. That's why I was getting so anxious."

The next few hours were a mad whirl. They called the doctor and found Mary Lou's bag, then had to get Charlie, cast and all, into Hope's wagon. Since the two of them wouldn't be separated, Mary Lou eased herself in beside him.

Then there was the craziness admitting them to the hospital—getting wheelchairs for both Mary Lou and Charlie and getting them to Delivery. Not to mention persuading the intern in charge that a blind man in a wheelchair could still be an effective labor coach.

Pete's temper mounted at each delay, but luckily, before it blew, Mary Lou's regular doctor arrived. Suddenly both the Riverses were whisked away and there was only Hope and Pete left.

Pete didn't need to look at her to know she was worn out. He felt as limp as an old feed sack himself.

"Let's sit down," he said. "I hear these things take time."

She was avoiding his eyes. The closeness he'd felt back there at the house had vanished. Now all he could think about was that night he'd walked away from her room. Away from her.

She sank down onto a couch. "Yes," she said. "Babies usually do take quite a while."

He let himself down beside her, and the next thing he knew he was holding her hand again.

"Sorry about the long drive," he said, "but I'm sure glad you were here. I don't know how I'd have managed it alone."

"Me, either." She gave him a weak little smile. "You did a fine job."

The warmth inside him spread. There was no denying it. What she thought of him mattered. It mattered a lot.

He could feel the warmth of her body. It reached out to him, calling for his touch. He held on to her hand. "Do you still think I did the right thing? I mean, telling her probably brought the baby on."

She turned to look at him, her eyes wide. "I really don't think that's the case, Pete. But even if it is, I still think it was the right thing. Don't you?"

He shrugged. "I don't know anymore. If something goes wrong..."

For a second he felt again the awful tearing pain of Annie's loss. He sighed. "If something goes wrong, it'll be my fault."

Her fingers were warm in his, her grip comforting. "Nothing's going to go wrong."

"I wish I was sure." He sighed and ran his free hand through his hair. "It's a bad habit I've got—telling people what to do with their lives."

He could still see Annie's face, hear her saying, "You're not God."

"I hadn't noticed," Hope said, her smile warm. "But shouldn't a person do that sometimes? I mean, if you see someone doing something wrong and you know it, shouldn't you try to stop them? Especially when it's someone you care about," she added softly.

"That's what I used to think." Now, he thought, now was the time to tell her that he knew. To tell her to get out of bullfighting while she was still in one piece.

"But," she went on, "how can we tell what's right and what's wrong? Especially for someone else. Charlie thought it was right to protect Mary Lou. For all we know, he could have been right."

Panic welled up in him, tightening his throat and his chest. He couldn't tell her. He could see that now. She was a grown woman with the right to do as she pleased. Even if what she was doing was tearing him up inside. Even if it was so dangerous he could hardly stand it.

"So we're right back where we started," he said carefully, finally managing to get the words out. "With no answers."

"I guess so."

The time passed slowly, the long afternoon hours dragging on and on. For a while they talked ranch business. Then Hope said, "I'm getting so sleepy. I think I'll just lean my head back for a while."

"Sure. Go ahead."

She fell asleep quickly, her head tilting sideways. He moved closer, letting it come to rest on his shoulder. She sighed deeply and arranged herself against him.

He sat that way through the rest of the long afternoon, hardly daring to breathe for fear of waking her, facing the hard and difficult truth. And coming to the painful conclusion.

The doctor came out just before six. "Waiting for Mrs. Rivers?"

"Here," Pete answered, his heart in his throat.

The sound of the doctor's voice roused Hope. She looked up sleepily.

"Mrs. Rivers has a girl. Mother and daughter are doing fine. But the father—" He shook his head.

Hope came awake with a sickening jerk. She scrambled to her feet, with Pete right beside her. "Charlie. What's wrong with Charlie?"

The doctor frowned. "He claims he was blind."

"*Was* blind? What do you mean?"

"Well, whatever he was when he came in, he's seeing now. He told me he had a corneal abrasion but it was healed and he still couldn't see." The doctor looked thoughtful. "Could be the loss of sight was hysterical." He smiled. "Not that it matters now."

Hope turned to Pete. "I can't believe it. Charlie can see! Oh, Pete, it's so wonderful, isn't it?"

In her joy she forgot herself and threw her arms around him. She felt that second, that sobering second of hesitation, before he closed his arms around her. But she tried not to think about it. She thought instead about Charlie and about how everything had turned out in the end.

Finally she eased herself out of the comfort of his arms. "Where is Charlie?" she asked the doctor.

"He'll be out in a few minutes. Once we got Mrs. Rivers settled, he insisted on having some crutches."

The doctor smiled. "He says he's not riding any wheelchair when he has two perfectly good eyes."

As the doctor walked away, Hope turned to the man beside her. "Isn't it wonderful?"

"Yeah, it's great." He looked down at his watch. "Listen, Hope, I've got to run. Thanks for helping with this."

"But—" She stared at him, hardly able to believe her ears. How could he be leaving now? So suddenly. "Don't you want to see the baby?"

A spasm of pain crossed his face and was gone. "Can't," he said. "Tell Charlie I'm sorry. Mary Lou, too."

He took a backward step, as though he thought she might try to hang on to him.

"Pete, I—"

"Listen, I've got to tell you something. I'm sorry if I gave you the wrong idea the other night." His face reddened. "Truth is... I'm not... I've got no business getting serious about a woman."

"I don't understand." Her eyes searched his face, looking for something, some reason this was happening. All she saw was pain.

"I'm trying to tell you. This is it."

She echoed his words, trying to make sense of them. "This is what?"

"We're... over. I won't be calling you again. Seeing you. There's nothing between us."

"But Pete—"

"Nothing," he repeated, his voice hoarse. "Good-bye, Hope."

She took a step forward, but even as she moved she knew there was no stopping him. Not with that look in his eyes. There would be no miracle for them.

By a great effort of will she kept herself from calling after him, from bursting into tears. But she couldn't keep herself from whispering, "Goodbye, Pete. I love you."

Chapter Eleven

As July melted into August, the endless series of Montana towns left little imprint on Hope's mind. Stanford, Helena, Glasgow. Great Falls, Sidney, Scobey. Back and forth across the state, Hope followed the circuit, down one prairie road after another.

By mid-August she was exhausted. Three successive rodeos lay ahead of her, covering an eight-day span, the last two almost at opposite ends of the state.

But she would handle them, she told herself. Just as she handled the bulls, just as she handled the pain that was now a continual part of her life.

When Pete hadn't showed up at Stanford she'd almost welcomed his absence. It would be hard to remember to act like Hobie when her mind was screaming for answers, her body longing for his touch.

But when Pete didn't show at Helena and then at Glasgow, she began to worry. There were so many things that could happen to a man. She knew that far too well.

Then the word came along the grapevine. Pete Hamilton had gone to Houston to spend some time with his folks. So she hid her grief behind her clown's face and went to meet the bulls.

The money piled up in the bank. She figured that after the Labor Day show at Dillon she could quit the circuit. There would be enough for the new bull, and even some to spare.

Much as she wanted to do it, the thought of quitting brought fresh pain. Once off the circuit she would lose all chance of seeing Pete again.

By the time she reached Kalispell on the twentieth she'd been on the road for six straight days. She was worn out, mentally and physically. When she got to her room, she tossed her case on one bed and collapsed on the other.

She had dealt with Clint's loss—mostly because she'd had to—but that had been different. She'd had Claire and Matt. And the memories. She'd had the security of knowing Clint had loved her.

With Pete there had really been very little. And yet there'd been the promise of so much. It was losing that promise that hurt the most.

But Pete was gone. He was out there somewhere. Probably looking for another woman. One who could give him what she so obviously couldn't. That made the hurt even worse.

The phone shrilled and she jumped. "Hello."

"Hi, Hope. This is Charlie."

"Charlie Rivers?"

"Yeah, I'm here in Kalispell."

"You're not—"

"Yeah, I'm out of my cast. Riding again."

She clamped her mouth shut. Charlie's decisions were his own to make. He was not her child.

"But that's not why I called you."

"The baby? Mary Lou?" Her mind went immediately to thoughts of disaster.

"Whoa! Slow down. They're both fine."

There was a pause.

"The reason I called is—I heard Pete's back. He's announcing tonight. And I thought you ought to know. I mean, after what you told us about the two of you that day in the hospital, I didn't want you to walk in cold...and hear him talking. Not when you've got to face the bulls."

Her heart rose up in her throat. For a second she wanted to run, wanted not to have to see him again. But she knew that was impossible.

Hobie Brown had responsibilities. She needed his last paychecks. But most important of all, she wanted, needed, to see Pete, to know that he was all right.

"Thanks, Charlie. You're a good friend."

Charlie's chuckle was a little forced. "Hey, look who's talking. Listen, are you gonna be okay? I mean, you got Old Devil Eyes out there tonight."

"I'll be okay." She made her voice firm. "But thanks for the warning."

Of course she would be okay. She put the phone back in the cradle. When she was in the arena, facing a bull, she kept everything else out of her mind. Actually, that was the only time her thoughts were free of Pete, of the pain of their last goodbye.

She turned her face into the pillow and let the tears come. It was better to cry now. Later there would be no time for tears.

That evening she went to the arena early. She wanted to give herself time to get used to hearing his voice again.

Old Devil Eyes had sent another cowboy to the hospital just last week. But that hadn't stopped the rest of them. They were all determined to ride the brute. And she had to be in her best form to protect them when they hit the dirt.

Staring out into the arena, Hope sighed. She had never understood the excessive concern about rodeo animals. Rodeo stock had a really good life. Nobody was going to mistreat an animal worth thousands of dollars.

It was the human stock that took the beating. Broken arms and legs, taped ribs and wrists and knees.

Injuries were the life of a rodeo cowboy. And occasionally the death.

She was glad Pete was out of that end of it. Rodeo competition was a young man's game. At thirty a man was through competing—or should be.

The bronc in the arena "sunfished," all four legs leaving the ground, his belly turning toward the sun. The crowd roared as the cowboy kept his seat. But Hope felt no thrill of excitement, no surge of joy at a job well done.

She stood there, letting the sound of Pete's voice wash over her. She'd hoped it might soothe her, make her feel a little better. But it didn't work that way.

Just the sound wasn't enough. She longed to hear him say her name, to take back those awful words of farewell.

She shoved her hands deep into the pockets of her baggy pants. There wasn't much hope of that. He'd made things real clear. There was nothing between them. Nothing.

That time on the prairie, that night in her motel room—they meant nothing to him.

That was hard to believe. But Pete wasn't a man to lie. He valued the truth.

For the thousandth time she wondered if he had somehow discovered that she was Hobie. But it wasn't like him just to walk away. Pete was a man who confronted his demons.

The bronc riding was over, and a specialty act galloped into the arena. Girls in dazzling costumes rode standing up, straddled three horses, did somersaults.

Hope watched it all, not really seeing any of it. And then her body went on the alert. It knew *he* was nearby. And she knew, too, in that moment of deep awareness, that this was what she'd been hoping for. If he wouldn't talk to Hope, maybe he would talk to Hobie.

"Evening, Hobie."

"Evening, boss." She went silent then, staring at the display of horsemanship in the arena.

He put his elbows on the railing and leaned beside her, his shoulder against hers. It was madness, he knew. He should have stayed in Houston. He'd made the right decision that day in the hospital. To get out of her life before he messed it up the way he had Annie's.

Sure, the thing with Charlie had worked out. But that had been a fluke, a rarity. He'd known he couldn't go on watching her fight the bulls. And he'd known he had no right to stop her. So he'd done the only thing left to do—he'd cut and run.

He'd stayed away a whole month. He'd figured she would be over him by now. But he'd missed the circuit. It was the only life he knew.

Between missing her and missing the rodeo he'd nearly gone crazy. So he'd come back.

But the minute he'd spotted that curly yellow wig he knew he'd been fooling himself. It wasn't the circuit that had been calling him back. It was her.

For the first time he really understood rodeo wives. He knew now why they wanted to be there to see it all. Nothing was worse than waiting—ready for that terrifying knock on the door. They were never really sure whether the ringing phone would be the voice of a loved one or bad news.

So he'd come back. Not to change things between them. He knew she was better off without him. But just to be there. To know.

"I hear Charlie's riding again," he said, more to make conversation than anything else.

"Yeah. Too bad."

"Too bad?"

"The man's got a family. He ought to think about that."

That struck him as strange. She had that kid, Matt, as solid a boy as a man could ask for, though he was hurting because she was gone so much. And she was here, letting him hurt.

"Lots of people have families," he said. "They've still got to work."

"I know."

The misery in her voice stabbed at him. What was making her feel so bad?

"Still," he went on, "it's important for kids to spend time with their parents." He sensed her stiffening, but he went on. This wasn't telling her what to do. This was just a subtle way of making her think. "Sometimes the best kids get mixed up. If their folks don't give them enough attention, that is."

For a moment there was silence. "I suppose so," she said finally. "But a kid ought to be able to understand things, too. Being a parent isn't easy. At least it doesn't look to me like it would be."

"Not to me, either," he said. But the image of the boy's face stayed in his mind. The kid needed a father. He wondered if the boy knew his mother was fighting bulls. Probably not. He wasn't the kind to keep something that exciting to himself. He would want to be there, seeing it done.

Seeing it done. The words echoed again and again in his mind.

He straightened. "Well," he said, "guess I'd better get back to work." He lingered another second, just enjoying being near her. There wouldn't be much more of that. "See you around, Hobie."

"So long."

Hope didn't turn. She was afraid that even the heavy face paint couldn't hide her pain. And his words had made her think again of Matt.

They'd taken a long ride together after she'd gotten back from the hospital. She explained to him again about Charlie's blindness, about both Charlie and Mary Lou being without parents.

His eyes had filled with tears when she'd said, "I know what that feels like, honey. I had to be there for them. For a little while, at least."

They rode for a while longer. Then Matt cleared his throat. "Mom, I'm sorry I kicked up such a fuss. And . . . and that I said those awful things to you."

He brushed at his eyes. "It's just . . . you've been gone so much this summer. Gram's great, but she's not you. And . . . and I still miss Dad."

"Of course you do, Matt. We all do. But the summer will soon be over. Then I'll be home all the time again."

"Promise?"

"I promise."

"Great." He rubbed his pinto's neck. "Say, will that Pete Hamilton be coming around again?"

Hope's heart contracted painfully. "I don't think so. He's a busy man."

Matt's face fell. "That's too bad. I liked him."

She was glad Matt had said that, and yet it hurt, too. Staring out into the arena, Hope recognized what she'd hidden from herself that day on their ride. Matt had obviously hoped that Pete would become something more than a friend. Maybe even a stepfather.

She sighed. It was hard giving up dreams like that. She woke nights and lay there thinking of Pete, seeing his face, feeling his touch. And sometimes she cried.

But in the morning she got up and went on with her life. She still had the Circle C. And Matt and Claire. She was a lucky woman.

Hope straightened when she heard Pete's voice over the loudspeaker. Pete was saying, "And now, folks, for our bullriding events. Here's our bullfighting clown, Hobie Brown. He may be a little fellow, but Hobie Brown sure has guts."

Hope pranced into the arena, waving her huge orange hankie at the crowd. Somewhere in the back of her mind was a flicker of concern about Charlie. His leg must have just come out of the cast. She knew what the doctors must have told him—just as she knew that most cowboys would go right ahead and ignore the good advice.

But she kept her attention focused on the bulls in the arena. Finally she heard Pete say, "The next bull up is Old Devil Eyes, one of the meanest critters on the face of this earth. And riding him is Charlie Rivers, out of Butte. Charlie's a little behind on points this season. He broke his leg a while back, riding this same ornery cuss. And now, folks, let's watch Charlie do his stuff."

Hope waited, every muscle tensed, as the bull shot out of the chute. He was giving Charlie a wild ride, but Charlie was sticking it out.

Hope felt a surge of pride that surprised her. Seen objectively, Charlie's decision to ride again seemed foolish. But she knew that for Charlie it was the only decision to make. If he let an injury—or a bull—drive him out of competition he would feel himself less a man. For the first time Hope felt this on a gut level and understood it with her heart.

The buzzer sounded and Charlie hit the ground feet first. Hope was there instantly, darting between him and the bull while he rolled to one side. He was on his feet right away, though, raising his hands high in a victory sign to the crowd.

The bull tossed his head, lowered his wicked curved horns. Hope drew in a breath and held it while she waited. The bull pawed the ground. She mimicked his actions, sending the crowd into gales of laughter. For a second more, Hope and the bull faced each other.

Hope heaved a sigh of relief when he seemed to think better of trying for her today. She turned her attention to the next rider.

It was late when she got back to the motel. Charlie had waylaid her with pictures of the baby. But she was glad. Seeing his happiness had eased some of her pain.

"Did you ever think about telling Pete the truth?" Charlie asked as they sat over coffee.

"Many times," she replied. "But I was afraid. And then he said some things that scared me even more. Anyway, it doesn't matter. It's all over. There's nothing between us."

"It just seems funny to me," Charlie said. "I mean, you guys made me tell Mary Lou the truth."

"That was Pete's idea, not mine."

Charlie persisted. "But you thought he was right."

"Yes, I did." She sighed. "It's no use, Charlie. Whatever went wrong can't be fixed." She pushed her cup to one side. "It's been nice talking to you. Tell Mary Lou hello for me. But now I've got to get to bed. So do you if you're going to ride tomorrow."

They parted with promises to get together soon. And then Hope lay in the huge motel bed, wide-awake and exhausted.

One more day, she told herself. One more day here in Kalispell. A couple days off before Missoula, and ten days between Missoula and the Labor Day show at Dillon. She just had to hang on a little longer and she would be home safe—or at least home with enough money for the new bull.

This time the dream had no hazy edges. Every face, every piece of equipment, was etched crystal clear.

She stood in the center of the arena, facing the bull. It was Old Devil Eyes, of course. But this time the arena was full of people. Not in the stands, but down there with her.

Mary Lou, the baby in her arms, stood beside a grinning Charlie. Matt and Claire, hand in hand, stood waiting. And Pete. Pete was there, too.

But they all stood on the other side of the bull. All beyond her reach.

The bull snorted, his nostrils flaring. Her stomach lurched, and she tasted bile.

Behind Old Devil Eyes, Pete held out his hands to her. Matt and Claire and Charlie and Mary Lou did the same. "Come to us," Pete called. "Come to us, Hope."

"I want to, but I can't." Couldn't they see? "The bull—he's in the way."

"Forget the bull," Charlie called. "Forget him and come to us."

"But he's in the way."

"Mom." Matt's voice was so real. "Please, Mom, come to us. Leave the bulls alone."

The bull was still eyeing her. Hope's mind raced. How could she do as they asked? If she went to them the bull would follow.

But she wanted it so much—to be safe with the ones she loved. "Help me," she cried. "Show me how to—"

She woke with a sob in her throat and lay there shaking. What a strange dream.

She puzzled over it for a while before she fell back asleep. And it was on her mind when she went to the arena the next morning.

Chapter Twelve

The Friday-night crowd was really big. Hundreds of people devoured hot dogs and hamburgers, stickied themselves with cotton candy and candied apples, chomped caramel corn and buttered popcorn. And in between they hooted and hollered, having themselves a grand old time.

Hope did her work mechanically, the way she did everything these days. Her biggest feeling was one of relief that Charlie hadn't drawn Old Devil Eyes again so soon.

That bull was getting to be a real problem, for her, as well as for Charlie. It was bad enough to face Old Devil Eyes in reality. At least there she had some control. It wasn't the way it was in her dream world, where anything and everything could happen.

While she waited for another bull to come out of the chute, Hope looked over the crowd. It was a big crowd, full of laughing, excited kids. A group near the front caught her eye. At this time of the year, hopefully, they wouldn't have any firecrackers.

Her eyes continued to roam the stands, then swung back. It couldn't be, but that boy looked exactly like Matt. And beside him—that looked like his friend Jimmy.

Hope's heart pounded in her throat. Her mind was playing tricks on her, she told herself. Matt couldn't be there. He was safe at the Circle C.

"And now, ladies and gentlemen," Pete said, "we have the biggest treat of the evening—Harry Carson, out of Mesquite, up on Old Devil Eyes."

Hope tore her gaze away from the crowd. Forget Matt. Forget Pete. Forget everything but the bull that any second now would be charging out of that chute with murder in his heart.

And he came, trying his darnedest to unseat the rider. Hope counted under her breath. One thousand one. One thousand two. One thousand three.

That was all it took. Harry Carson came unseated.

The crowd gasped. His hand was hung up in the rigging, and the bull whipped him around.

Hope went right into action. She ran to the bull, actually yanking at his horn to get his attention. The crowd roared as his head swung toward her and he stood still.

She faced the bull, eyeball-to-eyeball with him. "Just stand there," she crooned. "Just stand there for one more little minute." And he did.

Unbelievably, the bull continued to stare at her. And then Harry Carson was loose and lighting out for the fence.

Hope took a deep breath.

The bull snorted, then lunged toward her, his evil eyes glowing with hatred. She sidestepped him. The bull... the bull was all that mattered. She had to remember that.

But now, superimposed over the bull's bulk, she saw Matt's face, his mouth open in fright, calling to her as he had in that last dream.

She shook her head. She couldn't be thinking of dreams now. It was too dangerous.

And then her foot hit a treacherous pebble half buried in the sawdust. Her ankle turned and she faltered, struggling to keep her balance.

In that instant the bull lunged again. She tried to throw herself to one side, out of his way, but she didn't quite make it. One huge horn hit her shoulder a glancing blow. She tried to roll with it, to minimize her landing the way Clint had taught her.

But she hit the sawdust so hard that the breath shot from her body. Even as she struggled to pull air into her tortured lungs, she knew she might never draw another breath. Old Devil Eyes had sharp hooves, too. He would he just as happy to trample the life out of her. But she couldn't move.

She fought for air, trying to pull in her arms and legs, to curl herself into a protective ball. But this could be the end of everything. *I'm sorry, Matt,* she thought. *Sorry to leave you like this.*

The thought made her fight even harder for air. She couldn't leave Matt. It would be too much for him.

As the stillness settled over her she realized that she could miraculously breathe again.

And over the roar of the crowd she heard the welcome sound of Charlie's voice. "Hobie, Hobie!" he was calling. "You all right?"

She opened her eyes, and there was Charlie's worried face. It was a beautiful sight. "I . . . I think so." Slowly she unrolled herself, testing each arm and leg. "He . . . he just knocked the wind out of me," she said. "I'm okay."

Hands reached out to pull her to her feet and hold her steady while she got her bearings. Pete's voice came over the loudspeaker. "He's up, folks! Hobie Brown is up! And he looks okay."

Hope took one step, then another. Everything worked. Nothing pained. She grinned. "I'm okay, boys. I'm really okay. Thanks. Thanks a lot."

One of the pickup men frowned. "Hey, don't thank us. It was Charlie that chased the devil out."

Hope turned to him. "Thanks, Charlie."

The young cowboy's eyes were suspiciously bright, but he grinned. "Any time, Hobie. Any time at all."

They went back to their places then, as Pete called another bullrider coming out of the chute.

Her knees were shaky, but she did her job. She did so well that when the bullriding was over and she took her usual bows the crowd surged to its feet.

For a moment she felt a little of what Clint had tried so hard to explain to her. Pride in her work. Pride in a job well done. But she knew that without Charlie she wouldn't have been around to hear the applause.

Once she was out of the arena the reaction set in. She found a barrel and sat down hard to wait out the shakes. There was no doubt that she'd come within inches of death. Good old Charlie...

Gradually the trembling subsided. It was time to get back to the motel. There was still tomorrow's show to do, and the shows after that. And she needed her rest if she was to do them right.

Slowly she got to her feet and began the long walk to the parking lot. She was about a foot from her wagon when a figure came hurtling out of the shadows and threw itself on her. The impact almost knocked her over, and she struggled to disentangle herself. She struggled, until she heard the words, interspersed with sobs, and recognized Matt's voice.

"Mom," he was saying. "Oh, Mom. I thought you were a goner. That bull... I thought he had you."

"Easy, Matt. I'm okay." She smoothed his tousled hair. "I'm fine, honey. Take it easy."

It took him a while, sobs tearing through him, before he could quiet down. Finally he raised his head.

"That's what you've been doing all summer, fighting bulls." His voice rose accusingly. "And you didn't tell me."

He had a right to be angry. But she wanted him to understand. "I didn't want to worry you, Matt. We needed money for a new bull. And this was the fastest way to get it."

She opened the wagon door. "Get in and we'll talk about it."

Reluctantly he released his hold on her.

"You see," she said, climbing behind the wheel, "I remembered how scared I used to get. When I watched your daddy. I didn't want you to feel like that."

Matt's face hardened. "So you just went off without telling me. You could have been killed." He snapped his fingers. "Just like that. The bull was almost on you when that cowboy grabbed him by the tail."

Hope smiled. So that was how Charlie did it! She patted her son's hand. "That cowboy was Charlie Rivers. The one I stayed to help in Red Lodge. He was returning the favor."

Matt's face softened. "I still don't think it's right. You lied to me."

"Now, Matt—"

"You always say that not telling the truth is lying. Don't you?"

She couldn't see any way out of this. "Yes, Matt. But this is more complicated. I was trying to protect you."

"I'm not a baby. If you're going to do things like this, I've got a right to know." He reached out to take her hand. "You're all I've got left."

Her lower lip started to quiver, and she clamped down on it with her teeth. This was not the time for tears. "I'm careful, Matt. And it's not as dangerous as it looks. But I understand your being afraid for me. That's how I got to be a clown in the first place. I was afraid for your daddy. So he taught me what to do."

She squeezed the hand that held hers. "Then I wasn't afraid anymore."

Matt sniffled. "I don't see how Mr. Hamilton can let you do it. He knows you're my only—" He stopped suddenly and turned to stare at her. "Mr. Hamilton doesn't know. You lied to him, too!"

Hope's heart sank. He was right, of course. She *had* lied to Pete Hamilton, and all her fancy explanations couldn't change that fact.

She took a deep breath. "Matt, honey, sometimes grown-ups make mistakes, too. We needed the money to replace Sultan. No one would hire me when I went as a woman, so Gram suggested, and I agreed, that I could go in costume and let Mr. Hamilton think I was a man."

Matt shook his head. "Don't you mean any of those things you always say to me? About the truth being so important? About being true to yourself?"

"Yes, Matt, I meant them. And I guess the circumstances were no excuse. I just made a mistake. But I didn't see any other way." Poor Matt. She'd really let him down.

He looked at her thoughtfully. "Okay, you made a mistake. Now, how're you going to fix it?"

Hope sighed. Sometimes she thought they had taught him too well. But he was right. She'd done something wrong and she should do everything in her power to set it right. "How can I fix it for you?" she asked.

Matt's answer came instantly. "Get out of the arena."

"But the ranch—what if we lose it?"

Matt shook his head. "I don't care about the ranch." He hesitated. "At least not as much as I care about you."

"And your pony? What about him?"

He swallowed, but he went bravely on. "I'd give up everything I have," he said, "to get you away from the bulls."

"The season's almost over," Hope said. "There are just a few more rodeos to go. I was going to quit anyway."

"Please, Mom." There was desperation in his voice. "Please don't wait. Quit now."

For some reason she remembered the dream. It seemed almost like a sign. But this was her job. "Matt, I have a contract, responsibilities."

Matt shook his head. "Mr. Hamilton can get another clown." He paused, and his voice changed. "I can't get another mother."

He looked down at his lap. She could see he was about to break into tears again.

Hope knew then what she had to do. She couldn't let Matt live in terror. They would make do with the money she'd earned. "All right, Matt. I'll see about quitting."

Matt's smile warmed her heart. "That's great, Mom." He hesitated. "Are you going to fix it with him, too?"

She knew what he meant, but she asked anyway. "With who?"

"With Mr. Hamilton. You lied to him, too. He's a nice guy, Mom. He deserves better than that."

"You're right again, Matt. He does."

Hope put the key in the ignition. "By the way, what are you doing here?"

"Mr. Hamilton sent tickets. Enough for Jimmy and his folks. They're waiting, over there by the gate." He sent her an anxious look. "Don't be mad at me. Gram said I could come."

She patted his shoulder. "I'm not mad. But you'd better run along. Don't keep Jimmy's folks waiting. I'll see you at home."

"Okay." He gave her a long last look. "I love you, Mom."

"I love you, too, honey."

He was right, she thought as she watched him run to join Jimmy's family. This whole thing had been a big mistake. It was too late to fix it, but she could at least tell Pete the truth. She owed him that much.

The noisy crowd were filing out, laughing and jostling each other. Moving against the current, she made her way back into the arena.

Pete should still be up in the office, putting things to rights for the night.

It didn't take her long to reach the door, certainly not long enough to calm the pounding of her heart. For a second she stood there, gathering her courage. Then, finally, she knocked.

"Who is it?"

"Hobie."

"Door's unlocked, Hobie. Come on in."

He was standing with his back to the door, looking out the window at the emptying arena. He didn't turn. "Glad you're okay," he said. "I'd hate to lose a first-rate clown."

Her heart seemed permanently stuck in her throat. She swallowed over the lump it made. "I've got to talk to you about that."

"Okay." He still didn't turn. "Go ahead."

She wanted desperately to see his face, to gauge his reaction while she was telling him her story. But she was afraid to wait, afraid she would lose her nerve entirely. Once he knew the whole truth he wouldn't be talking to Hobie, anyway.

She took a deep breath. "I'm leaving the circuit."

She saw his shoulders stiffen, and she waited, but he still didn't turn.

"Sorry to hear that," he said finally. "But I expect you have a good reason."

"Actually, I have several." Her lower lip trembled, and she gnawed on it anxiously. "First off, I'm not Hobie Brown. I'm Hope Crenshaw." She yanked off the yellow wig and threw it on the desk. "I lied to you because I needed the job. But it was a mistake. Lying always is. And I'm sorry. More sorry than you'll ever know."

She knew she was rattling on, hardly making sense. But the sight of his broad, immovable back unnerved her. It was the visible symbol of his shutting her out. He might never look at her again.

She swallowed and went on. "I can't clown for you anymore. You didn't know, but the tickets you sent Matt . . . He came with his friend. And he recognized me. He . . . he wants me to stop fighting bulls." Her breath caught in a sob. "To stop lying."

"That's a good idea," Pete said, his voice hoarse, his back still to her. "A real good idea."

She pulled the orange hankie from her pocket and wiped at her tearstained face. Why didn't he turn around?

"There are some truths *I* owe *you*," he said, his voice husky. "I told you about Annie. A little. But I didn't tell you what her lying and cheating did to me. How I decided never to trust a woman again."

His shoulders shook. Finally he went on. "Her lying destroyed our marriage, our love."

Hope scrubbed at her face with the hankie. She didn't want to be Hobie the clown ever again. "I know

I was wrong," she repeated. "I said I'm sorry. There's nothing else I can do."

"Yes, there is."

His voice was strange, uneven. Her heart pounded in her throat. What was he talking about?

"You can marry me," he said. "And never lie to me again."

Hope's breath left her body in a whoosh of surprise. She couldn't possibly have heard him right. "Marry you?" she repeated, her voice faltering.

He turned then and came toward her. "Yes," he said. "Marry me."

She could hardly believe her eyes. The man was smiling.

He came right to her and took her in his arms. "Did you really think I didn't know?" He kissed her on the forehead. "I suspected the day you came to the office looking for work. And I knew for sure when I visited the ranch."

She could hardly believe this was happening. She leaned into his body, savoring the feel of it. "But how? How could you tell?"

He dropped a kiss on her lower lip. "That habit you have of gnawing on your lip. You did it that day in the office. And again when I was at the ranch."

Hope tilted her head and stared up at him. "You knew? And you didn't say anything?" She tried to look angry. "Pete Hamilton, you lied, too."

He grinned sheepishly. "Yeah. I made my share of mistakes. But I paid for them. I thought I was going to die every time you faced a bull." He hugged her fiercely. "I tell you, I'm never going to tease a rodeo wife again. I know what kind of hell they go through."

"Why didn't you tell me you knew? And fire me? I wouldn't have been able to work then."

"I wanted to. Lord knows, I wanted to. But Annie always said how I tried to run her life. That last time, before she drove off, that's what we fought about." He swallowed. "For a long time I thought I'd killed her."

"Oh, no!" She hugged him tighter.

"I'm all right. I got over it. I know Annie was responsible for herself."

She snuggled against his chest, trying to believe that it was all true, that it was really happening. Icy fingers slid down her spine at a memory. They'd been almost this close before, and then suddenly he'd been gone.

"Why—" She stumbled over the words. "Why did you leave me like that in the hospital? Why did you tell me there was nothing between us?"

He reached up and released the coil of her hair. "I figured I had to. I'd just interfered in Charlie's life. Yeah, I know, that time it worked out okay. But I was scared. It drove me half crazy, seeing you in there with the bulls. But I had no right to stop you. You hadn't trusted me with your secret."

"I wish I had," she whispered. "I wanted to, so many times. But I was afraid of losing you. At least as Hobie I got to be around you sometimes."

"Yeah, that about drove me crazy, too. All those little talks we had—Hobie and me. I wanted to kiss you worse than anything every time."

She giggled. "Wouldn't that have made some talk? But, Pete—" She had to follow through on this. "Are you sure? I mean, you sounded so certain that there was nothing between us."

"Oh, honey, I thought I could walk away from you. I thought it would be better for you." He sighed. "But I couldn't stay away. I needed to see you, even if it was just as Hobie."

He brushed her cheek with his lips. "I thought I could handle that. But tonight, when I saw you get knocked down and that bull going for you—"

He shuddered. "I knew it wasn't any use my trying to get away from you. I've got to learn to trust you. I love you too much to do anything else." He kissed the tip of her nose. "I'm sure glad you're quitting, though. I hoped—"

He paused, and she looked up. "What did you hope, Pete?"

He looked embarrassed. "I guess not telling a person something they have a right to know—that's lying, huh?"

She laughed. "I thought we'd pretty well established that."

He flushed. "Well, like you know, I sent Matt the tickets for tonight. And I *did* sort of hope..."

Hope gasped. "Pete Hamilton! You didn't! You didn't interfere again!" She tried to glare at him, but her heart was so full of happiness that she just couldn't do it. "You sent Matt those tickets hoping he'd recognize me!"

"Yeah." He grinned sheepishly. "He's a great kid. And, well he told me a lot that day at the ranch. I knew he was scared of losing you."

His hug threatened to cut off her breath.

"And believe me," he went on, "I knew just how he felt."

"Well, your interfering worked," Hope said. "This time, at least."

He shook his head. "I know that's no excuse. And I promise—"

She laid her finger across his lips. "None of that. Don't be making promises you can't keep."

He chuckled and gave her a weak smile. "I still can't believe you couldn't tell I knew you were Hobie. When you love someone, a little paint and some funny clothes don't hide who they are. I was counting on that when I sent Matt the tickets. I figured the kid would recognize his own mother."

He pulled her even tighter against him. "Say, honey, I've been thinking of getting off the circuit myself, settling down somewhere. What do you think?"

"Sounds good," Hope murmured against his chest. "Sounds real good."

"If it's okay with you, we'll announce our engagement during tomorrow's show."

Hope imagined Charlie's smiling face. And Matt's. And Claire's. "That'll be fine."

"Then when shall we start looking for a place to live?"

She raised her head, surprised. "What's wrong with the Circle C?"

"Nothing's wrong with it." He looked embarrassed again. "It's just that it was yours and Clint's. I thought maybe you wouldn't want—"

"Would you mind living there?" Hope asked. "Honest, now. This honesty thing has to go both ways."

He grinned. "I'll always be honest with you. No, Hope, I don't mind. I like the place. But there's the boy. And Clint's mom. We've got to think about them, you know. They have feelings, too."

"Don't you know that they like you?" She tilted her head to look up at him. "Remember, no lying now."

He grinned. "Well, the boy seemed to like me a lot. And she's been cordial enough. But..."

Hope's heart did a little jump. Surely he didn't think... She had to tell him before he went on, before she got any happier. "You know, of course, that Mom Crenshaw is part of the deal. She goes where I go. We're a family."

"Of course I know that." He squeezed her until she squealed in protest. "You'd better up your estimate of my smarts, honey. I'm not near as dumb a cowboy as you've been thinking."

"I never—"

He kissed her earlobe. "You'd better get it through that pretty head of yours that you're dealing with one brainy fellow here."

She hugged him. "Yes, sir. But there's just one more thing."

His frown of concern was instant.

"Honey," he asked, "what is it?"

"Well, you're asking me to give up a lot. The excitement. The challenge."

She smiled as his expression changed, as he caught on to her teasing.

"I mean, this is an exciting career I've got. Facing the bulls makes a person feel really alive."

Pete threw back his head and roared. "You want excitement?"

He brought his hands around her waist and lifted her until her face was even with his. "You want to feel alive? I'll give you all the excitement you can handle. You can count on it."

And with that he soundly kissed her.

*   *   *   *   *

COMING IN APRIL

NAVY BLUES
Debbie Macomber

Between the devil and the deep blue sea...

At Christmastime, Lieutenant Commander Steve Kyle finds his heart anchored by the past, so he vows to give his ex-wife wide berth. But Carol Kyle is quaffing milk and knitting tiny pastel blankets with a vengeance. She's determined to have a baby, and only one man will do as father-to-be—the only man she's ever loved...her own bullheaded ex-husband! Can the wall of bitterness protecting Steve's battered heart possibly withstand the hurricane force of his Navy wife's will?

You met Steve and Carol in NAVY WIFE (Special Edition #494)—you'll cheer for them in NAVY BLUES (Special Edition #518). (And as a bonus for NAVY WIFE fans, newlyweds Rush and Lindy Callaghan reveal a surprise of their own....)

Each book stands alone—together they're Debbie Macomber's most delightful duo to date! Don't miss

NAVY BLUES
Available in April,
only in *Silhouette Special Edition*.
Having the "blues" was never
so much fun!

SE518-1